FORTUNES TOLD

A VOYAGER'S GUIDE *to* LIFE *between* WORLDS

Copyright © 2025 PI & Other Tales, Inc.

All rights reserved. No part of this book may be reproduced
or transmitted in any form or by any means, electronic or mechanical,
including photocopying, recording or by any information storage and retrieval system,
without permission in writing from the Publisher,
except as permitted by copyright law.

David James Lennon asserts the moral right to be identified as
the author of this work.

Fortunes Told® is a registered trademark of David James Lennon in the
United Kingdom and other territories, used with permission.

First edition

ISBN 978-1-0684447-1-5
ISBN 978-1-0684447-3-9 Paperback

A CIP Catalogue Record for this book is available
from the British Library

First Published in the United Kingdom by
Adventures of the Persistently Impaired (...and Other Tales) Limited,
London W1W

a PI & Other Tales, Inc. company
www.fortunestold.co

Printed and Bound in the United Kingdom

To Mal, in hope for better fortunes for both of us
(in French or otherwise),
Alex, for his love for adventure,
Leonardo, the inspiration for the journey back.

and Tonto.

For a lifetime of companionship along the way.

Contents

Preface	iv
1 A City Wakes	1
2 Portobello Road	19
3 The Reading	31
4 A Storm Breaks	47
5 Familiar Strangers	61
6 The Magician's Trap	76
7 Court of Revelations	87
8 The Hermit's Shadow	103
9 Wheel of Fortune	116
10 The Tower Falls	138
11 A Star In The Storm	154
12 The Moon's Reflection	163
13 The Sun Rises	176
14 Fortunes Told	193
About the Author	207

Preface

I can recall the first time I stepped onto Kennington Park Road as clearly as the nights I sat alone in the neighbouring park's Rose Garden the following years' Christmas. Whilst what you are about to read is a work of fiction, like most fiction, a very large part of it is grounded in truth—real-life events that occurred from the autumn of 2023 until quite recently.

It is, best described, somewhat of a fictionalised autobiography of my own experiences and life in south London over the last eighteen months, comprised of excerpts taken from my diaries detailing adventures and misadventures alike.

For more on how this novel came to be, once read, visit https://behind.fortunestold.co.

1

A City Wakes

The sun rose high above the city, casting long shadows upon the pavement of Kennington Park Road. Lukas sat perched on the top step of his Victorian terrace house, a chipped mug warming his hands, the steam a fragile, fleeting sculpture against the crisp morning air. It was his first official day of freedom – the first day in almost a decade he hadn't been swept along in the relentless human tide towards the City. The morning air held London's distinctive perfume: damp stone, diesel fumes and something a little sweeter – perhaps lime blossom from the trees lining the street. A siren wailed in the distance, its cry melding with the hollow rumble of the Underground beneath his feet and the persistent chatter of sparrows in the eaves above. Lukas closed his eyes briefly, letting the sounds wash over him. The city had its own soundtrack – layered, complex and almost entirely unappreciated by most. Back at the record label, he'd once created a marketing campaign for a breakout pop single about urban loneliness. He'd spent hours crafting social media content that captured the artist's vulnerability against the backdrop of city life, finding ways to make her late-night wanderings through London streets feel both intimate and authentic. His director had called it "brilliantly atmospheric" right before laying off half the marketing team.

"Late, absolutely late," muttered a woman in a crisp navy suit as she hurried past, her heels striking a quick rhythm against the pavement. Her phone was pressed to her ear, her free hand clutching a takeaway coffee cup that sloshed precariously with each step. Until a few weeks ago, that had been him – racing against the tyranny of time, breakfast reduced to whatever could be consumed while speed-walking to the Tube station, headphones pumping a now-forgotten hit from what seemed equivalent to another world to keep his pace up.

A businessman in an impeccably tailored suit strode past, barking into his mobile: "Need those projections by nine, absolutely non-negotiable." His elbows were as sharp as his consonants, parting the morning crowd akin to a ship's prow through waves. Lukas remembered that tone, that urgent self-importance. He'd worn it equivalent to armour, believing it made him invincible. Until the day the label was absorbed by some ultra-conglomerate and terms such as "restructuring" and "synergistic streamlining" had turned music's last creative haven into another corporate battlefield.

"Beautiful morning, isn't it?" The words came from an elderly gentleman who had paused beside Lukas's steps. His silver hair caught the sunlight, as he hummed something reminiscent of Dusty Springfield between words. "First day of freedom, by any chance?"

Lukas blinked in surprise. "How did you know?"

The man's eyes crinkled with knowing amusement. "That look of peaceful defiance. Saw it in my own mirror the day I retired. Though I suspect you're a bit young for that particular milestone."

"Redundancy," Lukas explained, raising his mug in a small salute. "Or as my exit interview delicately phrased it, 'differences in direction due to the corporate restructuring.' Time to finally write my own stories instead of crafting ones for others."

A CITY WAKES

"Ah, wisdom comes at different ages to different souls," the man said, resuming his unhurried pace.

As the old man walked away, Lukas noticed something peculiar. The gentleman's shadow didn't move quite in sync with his body, trailing a half-second behind as if reluctant to follow. When it finally caught up at the corner, it rippled against the pavement, comparable to water disturbed by a thrown stone. Lukas blinked hard. When he looked again, the shadow behaved normally, though the air where the man had stood felt oddly charged.

The melody the man had been humming lingered in the air. The notes hovered at the threshold of hearing, occasionally shifting when he wasn't paying direct attention, moving from major to minor and back again. The music stirred something in him – a Sunday morning from last autumn. James at the stove, Fleetwood Mac filling their tiny Hackney flat, moving through the kitchen with unexpected grace for someone so methodical in everything else. He'd made those ridiculously precise pancakes, each one perfectly measured, while Lukas had lounged at the counter arguing that imperfection was the soul of art. They'd ended up trading tastes from the same fork, the pancakes growing cold as they'd kissed, tension dissolving into laughter.

Two students rushed past, their conversation a rapid-fire exchange in another language that reminded Lukas of his year abroad in Stockholm. Those twelve months at the indie label had shaped his approach to music marketing more than his entire marketing degree. He'd returned to London with campaign concepts that his manager had found "uncommercially innovative" – a somewhat backhanded compliment that had both stung and filled him with pride. The pair reminded him of his university days—running between venues with promotional flyers for campus bands, convincing reluctant bar owners to host experimental music nights, his fingers perpetually stained with cheap ink from the well-worn library printer. How many times had he felt that same vibration in his fingertips after watching James drum, the residual energy of music still resonating between them?

A young woman in a pencil skirt hurried by and Lukas noticed her mismatched socks – one navy, one a subtle shade of charcoal. It was the sort of detail he'd have completely missed when he was part of that same relentless stream, his mind already in the office before his body had arrived. As she passed, she gave him an odd, sidelong glance, as though his presence on his own doorstep was somehow unexpected.

The morning light caught the Victorian ironwork of his home. Having just moved in yesterday, he was struck by how the morning light transformed the ironwork into shadow-stories across the aged stone steps. Each curl and flourish resembled a character in some forgotten alphabet, spelling out stories of craftsmanship from a time when beauty was considered as essential as function. His gaze traced the ornate details, finding echoes of the elaborate band posters he'd once designed, where every visual element conveyed something about the music itself.

As he watched, the shadows cast by the ironwork appeared to shift independently of the light source. He had the disconcerting feeling that the house was observing him, studying him with patient curiosity. When he lifted his hand, the sensation stopped immediately, but the echo of that rhythm remained in his palm.

A harried mother wrestled a pram past, its occupant conducting a thorough investigation of every crack in the pavement while a toddler danced an impatient circuit around them, singing an improvised song about dinosaurs. The woman's phone was wedged between her shoulder and ear: "Yes, I know the meeting's at nine, I'm just— No, the nursery doesn't open until— Yes, I understand it's important, but—"

As the family passed, the toddler turned and stared directly at Lukas with wide, solemn eyes for an unsettling moment before resuming his dinosaur song as if nothing had happened. The mother gave Lukas a distracted smile and hurried on, continuing her phone conversation as they disappeared around the corner.

Lukas watched them disappear, remembering countless similar scenes from his morning commutes. How many human stories had he rushed past without seeing? How many moments of frustration and joy and ordinary magic had he missed while his mind was buried in marketing materials and promotional schedules and desperate attempts to keep the artistic integrity alive in a world increasingly driven by algorithms and market research?

A woman in a vibrant scarlet coat hurried past, her face illuminated by the glow of her earphones. "I know, I know!" she muttered, the words triggering a phantom anxiety in Lukas's chest – that familiar flutter of panic, the obsessive checking of watches, the stomach-churning fear of being even a minute behind schedule. As she passed, she suddenly paused and glanced back at him, brow furrowed in momentary confusion. After a brief, puzzled look, she shook her head slightly as if dismissing a thought and hurried away, disappearing into the steady stream of morning commuters.

But he wasn't part of that dance any more. He could sit here, watching the sun climb higher, feeling the stone steps warm beneath him, listening to the city's symphony of sounds. His coffee had cooled to the perfect drinking temperature, and he savoured each sip, letting the bitter warmth ground him in this moment. The liquid in his mug rippled though he hadn't moved. When he tilted the mug, the coffee hesitated before settling, as though the laws of physics had momentarily paused in deliberation. The taste had changed too, taking on subtle notes of cardamom and something older, more complex – as if time itself had steeped in his cup.

A lone pigeon strutted past, its iridescent feathers catching the light as it investigated a discarded wrapper. Behind it came an elderly gentleman walking with deliberate slowness, his tiny Scottish terrier sniffing inquisitively at Lukas's steps. Lukas leaned forward, offering his hand to the small creature. He'd always had a way with animals – a patience that James teased was inversely proportional to his attention span with people. The terrier sniffed his fingers tentatively before allowing a brief scratch behind the ears. Its owner nodded a curt good morning, his eyes meeting Lukas's with quiet understanding – they were both outside the current now, observers rather than participants in the great urban rush.

As man and dog continued their walk, Lukas could have sworn that the terrier's paw prints left small indentations that glowed with a soft amber light. He blinked and the pavement returned to normal, though a faint impression of something otherworldly lingered at the edges of his vision.

The stream of commuters began to thin as the morning aged. Lukas stretched his legs, feeling the rough texture of the stone through his jeans. A profound sense of peace settled over him, deep and uncomplicated. This was right. This was where he needed to be.

The late morning sun poured through the tall, sash windows of the living room, illuminating swirling dust motes and the chaotic landscape of half-unpacked boxes. Lukas paused from arranging books on the newly assembled shelves to watch James meticulously adjust his tie in the hallway mirror.

"You sure you don't need help?" James asked, his voice carrying that familiar note of concern masked as casual inquiry. "I could easily move my client meeting. The restoration plans for the Bloomsbury building could wait another day." He smoothed his tie for the third time – a nervous habit from his student days when he'd sit in Lukas's university flat, fingers fidgeting with drumsticks while Lukas played old Beatles records into the early hours and planned marketing campaigns for campus bands.

In those days, James had been just another architecture student with a secret passion for classicism in a department that worshipped modernism—and a surprisingly skilled drummer in one of the bands Lukas had been promoting. Lukas had found him in the university courtyard, sketching gargoyles while everyone else designed minimalist cubes. He'd been fascinated by someone who could appreciate both history and possibility – the same qualities Lukas sought in the artists whose stories he told through his marketing work.

"And miss your moment with the heritage committee? Absolutely not." Lukas crossed to straighten James's already perfectly straight collar, an excuse to breathe in his familiar scent of coffee and expensive aftershave. "Besides, I want to get to know this old house properly. Explore its… peculiarities."

James's eyebrow arched slightly at the word "peculiarities," a subtle tell that Lukas had long ago learned to recognise. It was the same look he'd given Lukas when he'd suggested they buy a flat in up-and-coming Hackney five years ago, before the area had become fashionable, or when Lukas had proposed they holiday in Kyoto during the rainy season because "the rain on temple roofs creates stories no travel brochure could capture." A mix of scepticism and indulgent affection that said, "I think you're slightly mad, but I'm intrigued anyway."

As James arched his eyebrow, the mirror's reflection briefly wavered, evocative of heat rising from summer asphalt. Just for a moment – so briefly he might have imagined it – Lukas caught a glimpse of something else reflected – not their hallway, but what appeared to be a grand ballroom with unfathomably high ceilings and crystal chandeliers. The vision lasted barely a second before disappearing, leaving a faint scent of beeswax and aged wood.

"Speaking of peculiarities," James said, picking up his leather portfolio case with a practised motion that spoke of a thousand similar mornings. His fingers traced the embossed initials – J.M. – a gift from

Lukas on their fifth anniversary. "Are you absolutely certain about this, Lukas? Leaving everything behind?" His brow furrowed with genuine concern. "The market's volatile, and your position at the label was secure…"

"James." Lukas pressed a gentle finger to his lips, a gesture that had become their shorthand for 'please stop worrying.' "We've been over this. The redundancy package was generous, I've saved carefully and…" He paused, struggling to articulate the gnawing emptiness that had been growing inside him with each corporate directive, each artistic compromise. "I need this. Need to remember who I am when I'm not defined as just another line on a spreadsheet to strike off. I need to find my own voice again".

"Just promise me you won't try setting up a recording studio in the basement without consulting me first. Remember what happened in the Hackney flat." James retorted.

As James mentioned the basement, Lukas felt a strange vibration beneath his feet, as though the house had shivered in response to the word. The sensation travelled up his spine, creating a pleasant tingling that lingered at the base of his skull for several seconds.

"That was entirely the neighbour's cat's fault, and I maintain my innocence to this day." When they'd tried to convert their spare bedroom into a practice space, their efforts at soundproofing had somehow created an acoustic anomaly that amplified rather than dampened sound. The neighbour's cat had wandered in while Lukas was practising piano, and its panicked escape had resulted in a noise complaint, a broken window, and an emergency visit to the vet. James had spent weeks smoothing over relations with the neighbours while Lukas had redesigned the entire setup.

"And yet somehow we still have that cat hair-covered microphone foam," James said with a wry smile, the kind that crinkled the corners of his eyes and softened his otherwise precise features. "Lurking in some box, waiting to traumatise our new neighbours' pets."

As if responding to his words, a box in the corner shifted slightly, though nothing was touching it. The cardboard bulged outward for a moment before settling back into shape. From inside came a sound resembling distant purring that faded after a few seconds.

A sharp knock interrupted them. Lukas opened the door to find Mrs. Patterson from next door, her silver hair arranged in an elegant coil, holding aloft a Victoria sponge cake on a delicate china plate.

"Welcome to the street, dears," she said, her voice warm and slightly musical. "Thought you might need sustenance. Moving is desperately thirsty work."

"Mrs. Patterson, you shouldn't have," Lukas said, accepting the cake gratefully. The scent of vanilla and sugar filled the air. "Please, come in. Though I should warn you, it's rather chaotic at the moment."

As the cake passed over the threshold, its aroma intensified, becoming almost intoxicating. Small golden motes appeared to rise from its surface, though when Lukas blinked, they appeared to be just ordinary steam.

"Oh, I remember moving day vividly," she said, navigating around a precarious tower of boxes marked

'VINYL - CHRONOLOGICAL - FRAGILE'

with surprising grace. Her eyes held a sparkle of mischief as she surveyed the room. "When my Harold and I moved in next door in '73, this whole row was practically condemned. Victorian architecture wasn't exactly fashionable then. But we fought for these houses. They're special, you know. They have... character."

As Mrs. Patterson spoke the word "character," Lukas felt the house respond. The floorboards creaked, the walls seemed to inhale subtly, and the temperature around Mrs. Patterson fluctuated—warming, then cooling, then warming again. He glanced at James, who continued the conversation without any sign of noticing these strange phenomena.

The chandelier above them chimed three gentle notes, though no breeze stirred its crystals. James checked his watch, a subtle movement that nonetheless spoke volumes.

"I really must dash. Lovely to see you, Mrs. Patterson." He kissed Lukas quickly, his lips lingering a half-second longer than necessary. "Don't overdo it, love. And please try to get the bedroom somewhat habitable? A functioning bed is rather essential."

As he turned to leave, Lukas caught a fleeting glimpse of something in James's expression – a shadow of anxiety perhaps or something deeper – something that reminded him of the night three years ago when they'd argued about Lukas's dream of starting his own music marketing consultancy. James had sketched an elaborate plan on napkins – timelines, budgets, risk assessments – his natural tendency to structure colliding with Lukas's impulse to leap. The argument had ended with a smashed glass and three days of silence, only broken when Lukas had found a business plan meticulously researched and presented on his desk. "Not now," the attached note had read, "but someday, when it's right." It had been both an apology and a promise – James's way of saying he believed in Lukas's dreams, even if his practical mind feared their timing.

Sometimes Lukas wondered if James's need for structure wasn't just organisation but a deeper anxiety – a need to reshape a chaotic world into something manageable, to transform unpredictability into order.

As the front door closed behind James, Lukas felt the house respond. The air pressure shifted slightly, the walls exhaled, and the dust motes rearranged themselves. For a fleeting second, the golden hour light streaming through the windows bent at angles that defied explanation, casting shadows that couldn't possibly match the furniture creating them.

After James's departure, a comfortable silence settled between Lukas and Mrs. Patterson. He found mismatched mugs for tea and they sat in the only two chairs he'd managed to unpack, creating a small island of domesticity in the surrounding chaos.

"Your young man seems... remarkably ordered," Mrs. Patterson observed, accepting her mug with a knowing smile.

Lukas laughed softly. "That's putting it mildly. James thrives on structure – spreadsheets, schedules, five-year plans. I've seen him rearrange an entire bookshelf because one volume was half an inch out of alignment. I'm a bit more... fluid."

"A free spirit?" Mrs. Patterson's eyes held a glint of something deeper than simple understanding. "This house will suit you, then. It has a way of... accommodating its owners. Revealing things, gradually." She gestured toward the built-in shelves where Lukas had been arranging his eclectic collection of music books, vintage album covers, and dog-eared notebooks filled with lyrics and promotional ideas.

As she pointed, Lukas could have sworn the books on the shelf rippled as water disturbed by a pebble. When he looked again, three volumes had changed position, though he distinctly remembered placing them differently.

"My Harold was a bit like your James – everything in its proper place" she said, wistfully. "He was convinced he'd organised his books alphabetically, yet somehow his favourites always seemed to migrate to the most accessible shelves. Claimed it was the house... being thoughtful." she remarked as her eyes tracked something over Lukas's shoulder with quiet interest.

"Houses do settle," Lukas said, attempting rationality despite a flutter of something like anticipation in his chest. "Creaks and groans, the natural movement of old foundations."

"Oh, it's more than that," Mrs. Patterson leaned forward in her chair, her voice dropping to a conspiratorial whisper. "These old houses... they absorb something of their inhabitants over the years. Similar to a recording, if you'll pardon the metaphor." She smiled, acknowledging his profession. "Harold always said he could hear music sometimes – as distant records playing, though we never owned a player."

The air around them thickened as she spoke, taking on a honey-like quality that bent the light. From somewhere deep within the house came a sound – three notes that might have been the opening of "Space Oddity," followed by seconds of perfect silence. When the silence ended, the air returned to normal, though the temperature had dropped noticeably.

A sound chimed somewhere deep within the house – a melodious, slightly off-key note that made Lukas frown. He hadn't unpacked any clocks yet.

"Oh my," Mrs. Patterson straightened suddenly. "Look at the time! I really must be going. But you absolutely must come round for tea soon. I have albums... photographs of the street from the seventies. Such transformations you wouldn't believe."

As she moved toward the door, Lukas had the peculiar sensation that her shadow separated briefly from her feet, lagging several steps behind before rejoining her at the threshold.

After she left, Lukas stood in the centre of the room, surrounded by the comfortable clutter of his half-unpacked life. The house felt both familiar and strangely alive, as a presence quietly observing him. He'd chosen it partly for the original Victorian features that James had rhapsodised about – the ornate crown mouldings, the authentic fireplaces – but also for the way sound moved through its spaces, creating natural reverberations that reminded him of concert halls with ideal acoustics.

He turned back to the bookshelves, determined to impose some order on at least this small corner of his new world. But he paused, eyes narrowing in concentration. Hadn't he just arranged that shelf? The books seemed... different. Slightly rearranged, as if someone had shifted their positions while he wasn't looking directly at them. He definitely remembered placing his dog-eared copy of *that* John Niven novel next to his well-worn edition of "Vinyl Revival: The Analogue Renaissance." Now they were separated by a slender volume he didn't even recognise.

The spine was faded, the title just barely legible: "Whispers Between Worlds." When he touched the unknown book, his fingers tingled strangely. The cover felt simultaneously ancient and unfathomably smooth, akin to stone that had been polished for millennia. Lukas reached for it, but a distant sound—the subtle creak of a floorboard—distracted him. He turned his head, listening intently. The house settled around him, the afternoon light shifting in ways that seemed both natural and slightly deliberate, creating new shadows across the floor. For an instant, he thought he caught movement at the edge of his vision—not something physical, but more akin to a shift in the quality of the air itself. Lukas turned back to the bookshelf, his eyes finding the spine again. But now the faded lettering read something different entirely: *Wind in the Willows*. "Strange", he thought, blinking hard and looking again. "I could have sworn"...

"Right," he muttered, his voice a little louder than strictly necessary in the growing quiet. "Let's see what secrets you're hiding, shall we?" The afternoon light shifted subtly, casting new shadows across the floor. As Lukas moved through the rooms, unpacking boxes with methodical determination, he couldn't shake the feeling that the house was observing him, assessing him. Each object he placed felt comparable to an offering, a small token of domesticity laid before some ancient, watchful presence.

As he unpacked his collection of vintage vinyl, he noticed that when he turned away, the records appeared to reorganise themselves. Each time he looked back at the shelf, albums had changed position, grouping themselves differently than how he'd arranged them. After the third rearrangement, he gave up and allowed the house's logic to prevail.

The late afternoon sun painted the living room in shades of amber and gold, casting long fingers of light through the tall windows. Dust motes danced in the beams resembling tiny constellations, moving in configurations that appeared almost... deliberate. The air held the lingering scent of old paper, lemon drizzle cake, and something else – something floral and elusive that he couldn't quite identify.

He held his copy of *Great Expectations,* its cover soft and yielding beneath his fingers from years of countless late night reads. As he moved to return it to its proper place, something caught his eye – a discrepancy in the shadows cast by the bookcase. For a brief moment, it stretched across the floor at an angle that defied natural explanation, far too long and distorted for the position of the sun. Lukas blinked hard, shaking his head. When he looked again, the shadow seemed normal, obedient to the ordinary laws of physics. But the unsettling feeling remained, evocative of a faint, discordant note in an otherwise familiar melody.

He moved to the window, seeking the grounding familiarity of the outside world. The street below appeared perfectly normal: buses trundled past, pedestrians walked their dogs, a ginger cat luxuriated in a patch of sunlight on a neighbouring windowsill. But when he turned back to face the room, the bookshelves appeared to loom slightly larger than before, their upper reaches disappearing into shadows that shouldn't exist in such a well-lit space.

Looking back outside, he had the unsettling impression that people were watching him. A woman pushed her child's pushchair with one hand while pointing up at his window with the other, leaning to whisper something to her companion. A man walking his dog stopped directly across the street, staring openly at Lukas's window before shaking his head and continuing on his way.

Closing his eyes, Lukas counted to ten – a childhood habit from when his father had taught him to count measures on the piano. When he opened them, the room had returned to its proper proportions. The shelves were their usual height, the shadows behaved as they should. It was as if the house had taken a deep breath and exhaled, returning to a state of perfect normality.

But the moment of strangeness lingered in his mind, comparable to the after-image of a camera flash or the phantom note that seems to hang in the air after a piano key is struck.

"Tea," he announced to the empty room, his voice deliberately steady. "Definitely time for another cup of tea."

In the kitchen, he filled the kettle, hand hovering over his favourite mug – the chipped blue one with the faded Regal Recordings logo, now defunct but forever immortalised in his collection of band shirts and memorabilia.

As he waited for the water to boil, his gaze was drawn to the kitchen tiles. For a fleeting moment, he could have sworn the arrangements were shifting, black and white squares rearranging themselves in his peripheral vision. When he focused directly on them, the tiles remained fixed, but when he deliberately looked away while maintaining peripheral awareness, they appeared to move.

He felt a wave of dizziness wash over him, as though the room were subtly rotating. The kettle clicked off with an abrupt mechanical sound that made him jump. Steam billowed upward, forming shapes that appeared almost... intentional, evocative of words forming and dissolving before he could read them. The steam dissipated after several seconds, leaving behind a scent that shifted between Earl Grey, jasmine, and something older and unidentifiable.

Night was falling now, the sky outside deepening to indigo. The house creaked and settled around him, but each sound conveyed more meaning than it should, as if the very walls were trying to speak. From upstairs came a soft thud, then another – resembling footsteps, except he was absolutely alone in the house. Wasn't he?

The telephone rang, making him start. James's name lit up the screen, a welcome anchor to normality.

"Just checking you haven't buried yourself under an avalanche of vinyl," James said, his voice warm with affectionate concern beneath the office background noise.

"Still excavating," Lukas replied, trying to keep his voice light despite the way the shadows in the corner of the room appeared to be deepening, moving with subtle purpose. "The house is... interesting."

"Interesting?" James's tone sharpened slightly. "What do you mean?"

As Lukas searched for words, the kitchen light flickered – not randomly, but in a distinct arrangement. The shadows in the corner formed what resembled a doorway for a few seconds before dissolving back into ordinary darkness. The temperature dropped noticeably, then returned to normal.

"Just... old house things. Creaks and groans. You know."

But did James know? Could he explain the way the rooms appeared to shift when he wasn't looking directly at them? The strange, unfathomable angles of the shadows? The books that moved of their own accord?

"Well, I've good news," James said, his voice brightening. "The heritage committee loved the restoration proposal. They've actually asked if we'd consider extending the scope to include the adjacent building. It would mean more work, but..." He paused, and Lukas could almost see him, sitting at his drafting table, fingers trailing over the intricate plans he created, the world reimagined according to his vision. It was what had drawn Lukas to him at university – that ability to see not just what was, but what could be. To transform reality through sheer force of imagination and will. In his own way, James was as much an artist as any musician Lukas had promoted, though he'd never accept the label.

"I'm proud of you," Lukas said, meaning it. "You've worked so hard on this."

"Get some rest," James said softly, the office sounds fading as he presumably moved to a quieter space. "I'll be home tomorrow. We can tackle the rest of the unpacking together."

After hanging up, Lukas stood for a while in the room, feeling the weight of the house's attention around him. The darkness outside pressed against the windows comparable to a living thing somewhere deep within the walls, something chimed midnight – though his phone clearly showed 10:47 PM.

He climbed the stairs slowly, each step feeling slightly... wrong, as if the risers were a fraction of an inch too high or too low. The staircase appeared to extend and contract with each step, as if the house were breathing around him.

The landing stretched before him, the wallpaper arrangement shifting at the edges of his vision. In the bedroom, he went through his nightly routine with deliberate normality – brushing teeth, washing face, changing into pyjamas. Each familiar action felt comparable to an anchor, a tether to the ordinary world.

Yet even these simple tasks felt somehow altered. The water from the tap ran in unusual spirals before behaving as it should. His reflection in the bathroom mirror appeared to move a fraction of a second after he did, as if time itself were slightly out of sync.

He crawled into bed, pulling the covers up tightly around him. But as he lay there in the darkening room, he couldn't shake the feeling that the shadows in the corners were deepening, growing, reaching out with tendrils of inky blackness. The house settled around him with sighs and whispers, sounds that might have been the natural noises of an old building – or might have been something else entirely.

As consciousness began to slip away, Lukas couldn't shake the feeling that when he opened his eyes again, the world he knew would be... different. In the silence of the night, as his breathing deepened and slowed, the house seemed to exhale, settling into itself. The shadows retreated to their corners, the wallpaper stilled its undefinable dance, and everything appeared perfectly normal once more.

But beneath the surface, in the spaces between reality and dream, something stirred. Something waited. And as the first light of dawn began to creep across the London sky, the house held its breath, poised on the cusp of revelation.

2

Portobello Road

The amplified buzz of a Saturday morning on Portobello Road usually invigorated Lukas. Today, however, the vibrant chaos felt wrong, comparable to a Dolly Parton record playing at slightly the wrong speed. He adjusted his worn leather jacket – a recent find from this very market – and touched his wallet for reassurance, trying to ignore the unnerving knot in his stomach.

Mr. Thompson's antique stall came into view, nestled between a display of vintage floral dresses and a collection of antique cameras. Thompson was typically a beacon of cheerful salesmanship, his weathered face a map of laugh lines that deepened whenever he shared stories about his treasures. His blue eyes would twinkle as he spun tales about Victorian compasses that had guided explorers through uncharted territories or Art Deco cocktail shakers that had graced the tables of Jazz Age speakeasies.

Lukas had spent countless Saturdays here over the years, not just buying but listening—finding unexpected inspiration in the histories of these objects. Thompson's passionate description of a navigator's compass had inspired Lukas to craft marketing copy for an indie band's debut album about exploration and discovery, which had helped secure them unexpected press coverage and a spot on a popular late-night show. Today, that conversation returned to him as he approached the stall—the way he'd incorporated Thompson's vivid descriptions into marketing materials that critics had described as "hauntingly directional"—one of the few campaigns where the label had allowed Lukas's personal writing style to remain intact.

But today, something was different. The old man stood rigidly behind his display of polished brass and copper, his normally relaxed shoulders tensed resembling coiled springs. His hands, usually steady as he polished his wares, clenched and unclenched at his sides. Even his familiar tweed waistcoat, typically worn with comfortable shabby elegance, appeared to hang awkwardly on his frame.

"Morning, Mr. Thompson," Lukas called, trying to inject some normality into the air. "About that Victorian compass you mentioned last week…" He remembered Thompson's animated description of its intricate workings, how the old man's eyes had lit up as he demonstrated the way its brass needle would spin and settle with unwavering precision.

Thompson's gaze snapped toward Lukas, then immediately away, as though the sight of him caused physical discomfort. The old man's fingers trembled as they arranged a set of brass doorknobs into a perfect circle—not the usual tidy row. Each knob was placed at exactly the same distance from its neighbours, creating a geometric precision that appeared both deliberate and unsettling.

"Not today," Thompson muttered, his voice barely audible over the market's hum. "Some things aren't meant to be found."

"I'm sorry?" Lukas leaned closer, uncertain he'd heard correctly. As he did, he noticed something odd about the arrangement of items on Thompson's stall. Usually, the man organised his wares chronologically or by function. Today, they appeared arranged in an unusual motif, as if communicating something he couldn't quite grasp.

"The compass points true north," Thompson whispered, his gaze darting nervously to the sky. "But what if north isn't where it should be today?" His fingers brushed against an ornate pocket watch. "Time feels wrong. Stretched thin in places. Too thick in others."

A prickle of unease ran down Lukas's spine. "Have I... done something to offend you?"

"Not yet," Thompson replied cryptically, arranging small brass ornaments in a motif that appeared deliberate yet incomprehensible. "But boundaries weaken. Things slip through. Someone's opened a door that should've stayed closed."

As a young couple approached the stall, Thompson underwent a startling transformation. His rigid posture melted into welcoming warmth, and a practised smile spread across his face, though it didn't quite reach his eyes. "Good morning, dears! Lovely day for antiquing, isn't it?" His voice dripped with honeyed charm, all traces of hostility vanished. "This Art Nouveau vase would look splendid in your sitting room. Just came in yesterday – belonged to a duchess, or so I'm told..."

The couple, oblivious to the previous exchange, began examining a Victorian photo album. Their casual banter about where to place it in their home appeared suddenly hollow, akin to actors reciting lines in an empty theatre.

Lukas stepped back, bewildered and slightly disturbed. The market crowd flowed around him, but their movements appeared subtly mechanical, their laughter a touch too loud, their conversations echoing oddly. A street musician's melody, usually a cheerful backdrop, now grated on his ears, the notes subtly discordant. What should have been a simple folk tune in D major kept slipping into passages that clashed with the underlying harmony.

Thompson abruptly looked up from his customers, catching Lukas's eye. For a brief moment, genuine concern flashed across his features. He mouthed something that resembled "Go home," before returning to his sales pitch.

The unease growing in Lukas's chest compelled him to move deeper into the market, as if seeking something that might explain this strange dissonance. The familiar layout of stalls appeared slightly off today – had that corner always been so sharp? Had these vendors always been spaced so far apart? He blinked, trying to recalibrate his sense of the space he'd visited countless times before.

The market's typical sounds felt oddly heightened today. Conversations blurred together into a disorienting hum, while the music from a nearby stall appeared to clash with the rhythm of footsteps. His senses felt strangely alert, picking up details he'd normally filter out.

Lukas reached out to steady himself against a stack of vintage records. The familiar touch of the vinyl sleeves usually brought comfort, but today they conveyed an unusual resonance. A David Bowie album on top caught his attention, its cover art suddenly striking him as oddly significant, though he couldn't articulate why.

Lukas quickened his pace, his earlier leisurely stroll turning into a near-jog. He weaved through the throng of tourists and locals, trying to shake the growing sense of disorientation. The faces around him appeared unusually attentive, their glances lingering slightly longer than felt comfortable.

A busker painted gold from head to toe nodded as he passed, the performer's intense stare following him through the crowd. Something about the blank expression beneath the metallic paint left Lukas unsettled.

The familiar layout of the market felt confusing today. He turned a corner he'd walked a hundred times before, momentarily disoriented to find a set of stalls he thought were in another section. The scent of street food appeared stronger than usual, almost cloying.

He finally slowed, breathless, in a quieter section of the market. Looking back, the market stretched behind him, normal in the bright sunlight, yet somehow not quite right. The shadows appeared darker than they should be in the mid-morning light. And somewhere nearby, a child's laughter rang out, briefly silencing the market's hum.

He found himself standing before number 291b Portobello Road, "Cassandra's Emporium of Collectible Curiosities." The shop had always been there, wedged between a trendy café and a bustling vintage clothing store, but somehow he'd never properly noticed it before. His mind's eye typically catalogued every shopfront for potential artist collaboration venues, yet this one had escaped his attention—almost as if it occupied a blind spot in his consciousness.

Today, however, it commanded his attention. The narrow store-front blended Victorian and Georgian elements, its architecture distinct yet somehow forgettable. The windows, usually cloudy with dust, appeared to have been recently cleaned, offering glimpses of shadowy objects inside. The heavy wooden door stood ajar, propped open by a small weathered stool. And on that stool sat a rather remarkable looking tortoise.

The ancient creature was utterly still, its wrinkled neck extended with quiet dignity. Its shell bore the marks of countless years, each plate telling its own story of time and travel. But it was the eyes that held Lukas transfixed – dark, intelligent, and observant in a way that felt almost unsettling. The tortoise appeared to study him with the careful consideration of a seasoned editor reviewing a manuscript.

"Extraordinary," a woman in a floral dress murmured, pausing briefly beside Lukas. "I've never noticed this place before, have you?" Her voice held the distracted quality of someone already planning the rest of their day.

"I've passed it," Lukas replied, though he couldn't recall ever truly seeing it. He'd walked this stretch of Portobello Road countless times, yet this particular store-front had never featured in his memories.

The woman had already moved on, swept along by the market's

relentless flow, her dress arrangement shifting as she disappeared into the crowd.

The tortoise hadn't moved, hadn't even blinked. Its attention remained fixed on Lukas with a focus that felt almost purposeful. A gentle breeze stirred the air, carrying the mingled scents of street food, exhaust fumes, and something else – something older, cleaner, with subtle hints of sandalwood and aged paper.

The market-goers continued to stream past, their chatter and laughter forming a familiar backdrop. Few of them appeared to notice 291b, their gazes sliding over it as if it were merely another unremarkable store-front among many. A group of tourists consulting a map walked past without a glance, their attention fixed on finding more famous market landmarks.

Lukas took a tentative step closer. The hand-painted sign above the door, "Cassandra's Emporium of Collectible Curiosities," was elegantly crafted but faded, the gold lettering catching occasional glints of sunlight. There was something about the typography that spoke of meticulous attention to detail, the kind that reminded him of vintage album covers from the 1960s that his grandmother had collected.

The tortoise's head turned slightly, following Lukas's movement. Something about its presence felt strangely grounding, a point of quiet certainty amid his increasingly confused perceptions of the market. This wasn't the sort of thing you saw every day at Portobello—a living, breathing guardian for a shop of curiosities.

A young couple brushed past, their shopping bags bumping against Lukas's legs. "Sorry, mate," the man called over his shoulder, barely sparing a glance for the shop or its unusual sentinel.

The tortoise shifted slightly, and Lukas's attention fell on a small brass plate attached to the stool's leg. The engraving read, simply: "Welcome, Seeker." Probably some clever marketing for the shop, he thought, though it struck him as oddly personal.

Beyond the tortoise, the open doorway revealed a dimly lit interior, a stark contrast to the bright day outside. Shadows played across shelves crowded with objects that Lukas couldn't quite make out from where he stood. The threshold felt comparable to a boundary between the familiar bustle of the market and something quieter, more contemplative.

"Are you just browsing, or did you come seeking something specific?" a voice asked from within, rich with a quiet confidence that drew his attention.

The tortoise's gaze remained fixed on him, patient and seemingly expectant.

"I'm not sure," Lukas replied honestly, surprised at his own admission. He was always searching for something—stories, connections, the perfect angle for whatever band the label had him promoting that week. But today felt different, his restlessness specific rather than general.

The market sounds began to fade as his attention focused on the shop entrance. From inside came the faint strains of music, played on what sounded akin to a vintage record player with its distinctive warm crackle. It reminded him of his grandmother, of rainy afternoons spent listening to old records in her attic, the music mixing with the patter of rain.

His grandmother had understood his unusual love of music from the beginning. "You feel music differently than others, little one," she'd told him when he was barely six, after he'd explained how certain songs created emotions and images in his mind. "You hear stories where others just hear notes." She'd nurtured this sensitivity, introducing him to her vast record collection years before his formal music education began.

The tortoise shifted slightly, its timeless eyes still watching him. The creature's presence was strangely compelling, drawing Lukas's attention despite the bustle of the market around them.

A sudden gust of wind whipped through the market, sending napkins flying from nearby café tables and causing awnings to flap noisily. The tortoise remained imperturbably still, as though existing in a bubble of calm.

Standing directly before the creature, Lukas could see the countless years mapped in its shell, each plate a testament to time and travel. The tortoise radiated an aura of profound age that made Lukas feel transient by comparison.

The shop beyond beckoned with the promise of stories waiting to be discovered. Lukas felt a familiar tingle—the same sensation he experienced when encountering a new band for the first time, a career with many stories waiting to be shaped. His writer's instinct, honed through years of finding the perfect angle to connect artists to people who'd love them most, whispered that there was something here worth exploring.

The music – distinctly Françoise Hardy, though he couldn't quite catch the title – drifted through the doorway as Lukas stepped across the threshold. The scent of sandalwood and old paper intensified, reminding him of record sleeves and liner notes from bygone eras.

The shop's interior was narrow but deep, with aisles between shelves creating a maze-like quality that made the space feel larger than the store-front suggested. Objects cluttered every surface – antique curios, vintage books, peculiar artefacts from what appeared to be various corners of the world. A glass display case held what looked like navigational instruments, while another showcased a collection of peculiar timepieces. A stuffed raven perched atop a globe with faded continents, its glass eyes catching the light as Lukas passed.

"Most people browse for twenty-three minutes before they find what they're looking for," a voice said from behind him.

Lukas turned to find a woman standing there, having approached silently despite the creaking floorboards. She wore a midnight blue dress that complemented her silver hair, which was swept up in an elegant style secured with what appeared to be antique hairpins. Her eyes were keen and observant, holding the depth of someone who had spent a lifetime watching people and collecting their stories.

"I'm Cassandra," she said, her accent cultured but difficult to place, hints of travel and different worlds within it. "Though you knew that from the sign, of course." A gentle smile played at the corners of her mouth.

Lukas extended his hand. "Lukas. I'm just…" he gestured vaguely, "exploring."

"Nobody ever comes in knowing exactly what they're seeking," Cassandra replied with that same knowing smile. "And yet, they usually find precisely what they need." She gestured to the tortoise, who had somehow made his way inside without Lukas noticing and had settled near a shadowy corner. "Tonto has excellent judgment about visitors. Been a fixture here for as long as I can remember, and, for as long as my grandfather George could too." She watched as the tortoise positioned himself more comfortably. "Some days I wonder who's really keeping who company."

The tortoise's timeless eyes fixed on Lukas, a hint of what almost looked like recognition in their depths.

"The tortoise… his name is Tonto?" Lukas asked, drawn by the ancient creature's steady presence.

"Indeed," Cassandra replied with evident fondness. "He's been around for quite some time, and, for as long as my grandfather George could too." She watched as the tortoise settled himself more comfortably. "Some days I wonder who's really keeping who company."

Beside Tonto, barely visible in the dimness, sat a simple wooden box on a shelf overflowing with peculiar artefacts. Lukas found himself drawn to it, his feet moving without conscious thought. The box was plain, unvarnished wood, marked only with the words "FORTUNES TOLD" in faded gold lettering.

The words sparked something in him— but he couldn't quite place what...Fortunes Told, not Fortunes *Sold* or Fortunes *Found*. The phrasing struck him as deliberate, a story waiting to be uncovered.

"How much?" he asked, his hands already reaching for the box. The wood grain felt smooth beneath his fingers, worn by hands that had touched it before.

Cassandra, now standing beside him with remarkable quietness for someone navigating a crowded shop, said, "The price depends on what you see in them." She watched his face with the careful attention of someone reading a complex text. "What draws you to these particular cards?"

As his fingers brushed against the box, a rumble of thunder echoed from outside, a stark contrast to the clear sky he'd seen moments before. The box felt warm in his hands, well-handled and comfortable.

When he opened it, the cards inside were unlike any tarot deck he'd seen before. The images were intricate and unusual, rendered with an artist's eye for meaningful detail. Each card appeared to contain a complete narrative, an entire world captured in a single frame.

"These aren't standard tarot cards," he said, noticing the unusual imagery and symbolism.

"Nothing in this shop is standard," Cassandra replied, her voice carrying quiet certainty. "Mass-produced things belong in other shops, and this isn't one of those, is it?" Her dress rustled softly as she moved to stand beside him, studying his reaction rather than the cards themselves.

The French music had shifted to a slower, more melancholic melody – Juliette Gréco now, singing about lost summers and fading memories. The song appeared to perfectly complement the moment, as if curated specifically for his thoughts.

Without hesitation, Lukas said, "Seven pounds and twenty-three pence." He knew, with quiet certainty, that this was the exact amount of money he had in his wallet. The price felt right somehow, evocative of the perfect word in a sentence that had previously felt incomplete.

Cassandra nodded, unsurprised. "A fair price for a storyteller's tool." Her eyes met his with quiet understanding. "These cards aren't about telling the future so much as revealing something about us we might otherwise miss."

The observation struck Lukas with unexpected force. Throughout his career in music, he'd always seen himself as a storyteller—someone who helped artists share their stories with audiences who needed to hear them. These cards, with their rich imagery and symbolic language, resonated with that same purpose.

"I've always been drawn to things that tell stories," he admitted, realising as he spoke that this was why he'd been feeling so adrift since losing his job. Without bands to promote, without stories to tell, he'd lost his sense of purpose. "I used to create marketing campaigns that told the stories behind the bands, not just their sound."

"Perhaps these cards will help you find new stories to tell," Cassandra suggested, her voice carrying no trace of the mystical salesmanship he might have expected. Instead, she sounded akin to a fellow professional recognising a tool of the trade. "Stories have power, especially the ones we tell ourselves."

As Lukas turned to leave, the cards secured in their wooden box, he noticed how the shop's narrow aisles created natural pathways through the cluttered space. The route back to the door appeared more straightforward than his wandering path in had been, as if the layout had been designed for smooth exits after purchases were made.

Cassandra's voice followed him as he approached the threshold. "I hope you find what you're looking for, Lukas."

He paused, turning back. "How did you know my name? I don't

think I mentioned it."

A soft laugh escaped her. "You introduced yourself when you came in. The mind plays tricks sometimes, especially in places filled with stories."

Had he? Lukas couldn't remember doing so, but the morning had been strange from the start, his attention fractured by Thompson's odd behaviour and the unsettling atmosphere of the market.

He stepped back into the bustle of Portobello Road, blinking in the sudden brightness. The sounds of commerce and conversation crashed over him after the muffled quiet of the shop. He looked down at the wooden box in his hands, running a finger over the gold lettering. When he looked back, Cassandra's Emporium appeared exactly as it had before—narrow, easy to miss, its windows reflecting the market crowds rather than revealing the treasures within. Tonto had disappeared from his post, presumably retreated into the shop's shadowy interior.

He might have dismissed the entire encounter as unremarkable had it not been for the weight of the box in his hands and the lingering scent of sandalwood clinging to his clothes. The market around him had returned to its normal rhythm—vendors calling to passing tourists, music blending with conversation, the organised chaos of a Saturday morning at Portobello Road.

As he tucked the box carefully into his jacket pocket, he felt the cards inside settling against his heart, a potential story waiting to be discovered. And in his mind, he could still see Tonto's timeless eyes, watching him with what had seemed like patient expectation.

A distant rumble of thunder echoed overhead, though the sky remained stubbornly, impossibly clear.

3

The Reading

The roof terrace floated like an island above Kennington's Victorian sprawl, a hard-won sanctuary between brick and sky. As evening approached, light spilled across London in sheets of amber and rose, catching on the spires of ancient churches and the gleaming glass of modern towers. From this height, the city seemed to breathe with its own peculiar rhythm – a living thing of stone and shadow, history and possibility.

Lukas adjusted a string of fairy lights with trembling fingers, their warm glow creating intimate pools of light against the gathering dusk. The terrace itself was a testament to his resourceful charm: mismatched chairs rescued from skips and charity shops formed an eclectic circle around a reclaimed cable drum that served as a table. Each piece told its own story of discovery and renewal, much like Lukas himself.

A collection of potted herbs created a living boundary between terrace and sky – basil, mint, and rosemary released their mingled fragrances into the evening air, their leaves whispering secrets in the breeze. A faded Persian rug, its intricate motifs softened by years of sun and rain, transformed the concrete floor into something almost magical. Its worn fibres held memories of countless conversations and shared laughter, promising more to come.

Across the rooftops, chimney pots stood like sentinels against the darkening sky. The spires of Victorian London pierced the soft pre-dusk light, their weathered stones holding centuries of secrets. Between them, glimpses of modern glass towers created a strange dialogue between past and present, a reminder that wonder could exist in both.

The view reminded Lukas of a soul album he'd promoted last year— the vintage sound reimagined for modern audiences, that beautiful intersection of nostalgia and innovation that had made the campaign so successful. The marketing photos had captured the artist against London's changing skyline, creating a visual conversation between eras that perfectly matched her timeless voice.

"You've outdone yourself, maestro," came a warm, familiar voice from the doorway.

Lukas turned to see James leaning against the frame, two bottles of wine cradled in his arms. There was something in James's expression – a mixture of affection and concern – that made Lukas's heart twist slightly. Since the visit to Portobello Market three days ago, Lukas had been distant, preoccupied with the strange wooden box and its contents. He'd said nothing to James about the encounter, unsure how to explain something he himself didn't understand.

"I needed this," Lukas admitted, taking one of the bottles and examining its label – an excellent premium brand, James's speciality. "A night with friends, under the sky instead of a studio ceiling."

James studied him, those perceptive eyes missing nothing. "You've been somewhere else these past few days," he said quietly, not accusatory but concerned. "Even when you're right next to me."

Lukas wanted to deny it, but the words caught in his throat. How could he explain the way the cards called to him from their wooden box? How they whispered when he was alone, promising revelations?

The way ordinary objects now held hidden meanings, shadows moved with subtle purpose?

"Just... adjusting," he said instead, opening the wine with practised motions. "Freedom takes some getting used to."

James nodded, though his expression suggested he wasn't entirely convinced. "Well, perhaps tonight will help ground you. Though I'm still not sure why you insisted on inviting Mike. You two haven't spoken properly since that disastrous session last year."

The memory made Lukas wince – Mike's drumming had been technically perfect but soulless on a track Lukas had been promoting. The argument that followed had ended their decade-long musical partnership and strained their even longer friendship.

But when Lukas had found the cards, Mike's face had immediately appeared in his mind, linked inexorably with tonight's gathering.

"Time to mend fences," Lukas said, pouring the wine into mismatched glasses. "Besides, he and Sarah always got along well."

That wasn't the whole truth. Since acquiring the cards, Lukas had experienced strange moments of intuition—brief, disorienting flashes where he appeared to see connections between people and events that hadn't yet occurred. Mike's face had appeared to him superimposed with an image from the Tarot deck, though he couldn't remember which card. The same had happened with Sarah and the others he'd invited. It was as if the cards were assembling their own audience through him.

The afternoon had been spent in meticulous preparation, each detail carefully considered. Glasses caught the fading light like liquid crystal, arranged beside bottles chosen with particular care – a crisp fruit cordial from New Zealand that tasted of summer storms and a rich blackcurrant pressé that held the evening's promise of transformation in its deep red depths.

Platters of carefully curated snacks dotted the space: plump green olives glistening in olive oil; sea salt crisps scattered like autumn leaves across vintage platters; a home-made dip of hummus and sun-dried tomatoes that caught the light like burnt amber.

In his pocket, the deck of cards from Cassandra's shop conveyed a subtle warmth against his thigh.

In the distance, thunder rumbled—a sound that made Lukas start, as no storms had been forecast. The dark clouds gathering on the horizon hadn't been there minutes ago, their edges tinged with an unnatural pearl-grey luminescence. James frowned at the sky, his methodical mind already calculating how quickly they could move everything indoors if necessary.

Sarah arrived first, her sharp heels clicking decisively across the terrace floor. Even in the softening evening light, her professional armour remained intact – crisp blazer, perfectly styled hair, ambition wrapped around her like an invisible cloak. She moved through the space with an interior designer's eye, mentally calculating spatial potential and design elements even as she smiled.

She'd been like this since university, when she'd organised their chaotic shared house with colour-coded labels and rearranged furniture for optimal flow. Back then, Lukas had created a quirky promotional campaign for her interior design student society, designing posters that captured her vision for transforming spaces. She'd pretended to hate them but had secretly kept one framed on her desk for years after.

Despite her professional polish, she'd remained fiercely loyal, standing by Lukas during that disastrous album launch when critics had savaged the band he'd been promoting and he'd nearly quit marketing altogether.

"Not bad, Lukas," she said, running a manicured finger along the fairy lights. "You've certainly put your stamp on the place. Although..." She tugged gently at a loose connection. "I'd get these checked. The wiring looks positively ancient."

"Always the optimist, aren't you, Sarah?" Lukas chuckled, grateful for her familiar bluntness. "Don't worry, I've got a spare set just in case."

Her gaze softened as she took in his nervous energy, the way his hands couldn't quite keep still. "It really is lovely up here," she conceded, accepting the glass of wine he offered. "I can see why you fought so hard for this place. It has... something."

The something she couldn't quite name hovered in the air between them, a prescience of things to come. The city sprawled below them like a tapestry of possibilities, lights beginning to flicker on in windows, each one a story waiting to be told.

Thunder sounded again, closer now. Sarah glanced at the gathering clouds with professional concern. "That wasn't in the forecast."

"Weather has its own agenda," Lukas replied, his hand unconsciously touching the pocket containing the cards.

Mike arrived next, his usual easy-going demeanour noticeably subdued. Where normally he brought laughter and light-hearted banter, tonight he carried shadows. His eyes darted around the terrace like trapped birds, fingers drumming an anxious rhythm against his thigh—not the steady, confident beat he'd kept when he and Lukas had first collaborated during university, Mike on drums and Lukas handling marketing for their short-lived band.

Even through his accounting career, Mike had maintained that innate sense of timing, that ability to find the underlying current in chaos—a quality that had made him both an excellent financial advisor to Lukas during the lean years and the perfect person to call at 3 a.m. when the world seemed to be falling apart.

The weight of unspoken words hung around his shoulders like a heavy cloak, a stark contrast to his typical buoyant presence. The tension between Mike and Lukas was immediately palpable, an unresolved chord hanging in the air. James subtly positioned himself between them, offering Mike a generous pour of wine with a warmth that deliberately ignored the strained atmosphere.

"Hey, man," Mike said, offering a quick hug that felt more like an attempt to steady himself than a greeting. "Thanks for inviting me. Needed a distraction." His voice carried an undertone of desperation that made Lukas's heart ache.

There was an awkward moment as Mike and Lukas regarded each other, a year's worth of silence stretching between them like a chasm. Then Mike glanced down at his glass, swirling the wine like he was searching for answers in its depths.

"Look, about last year's session—" he began.

Lukas shook his head. "Water under the bridge. I was precious about the band, you were right that the promotional angle needed tightening."

Mike's eyebrows rose in surprise. This was not the Lukas he remembered – the stubborn perfectionist who would argue for hours over a single marketing image. "You've... changed," he observed cautiously.

Had he? Lukas wasn't sure. But the cards in his pocket warmed at the acknowledgment, as if confirming something important had just transpired. A flash of lightning illuminated Mike's face momentarily, casting strange shadows that made him appear older, wiser, hanging suspended in a moment of decision.

Chloe and David appeared moments later, hand-in-hand, their arrival bringing a sense of balance to the gathering. They moved in perfect synchronisation, years of shared life evident in every unconscious gesture. Chloe, who'd been Lukas's first real advocate at the record label, still carried herself with that blend of artistic intuition and corporate savvy that had helped her rise from marketing assistant to executive producer in record time.

She'd fought legendary battles over Lukas's marketing campaigns, sometimes winning, sometimes losing, but never backing down. David, with his engineer's precision and innovative thinking, had become firm friends with Lukas after offering technical solutions to seemingly unfathomable promotional ideas—creating hidden sound installations in public spaces and designing interactive displays that translated music into visual motifs.

"Lukas, darling, this is absolutely charming," Chloe gushed, her eyes sparkling as she took in the terrace. "It's like a secret garden in the sky."

David nodded in agreement, his arm comfortably draped around her waist. "Though I hope those chairs are sturdier than they look," he added with a wink.

Another rumble of thunder, louder and more insistent. The gathering clouds now dominated half the sky, moving unnaturally fast toward them. The air grew thick with ozone and anticipation.

James quietly studied the assembled group, his analytical mind trying to understand why Lukas had brought this particular combination of people together tonight. Sarah with her designer's precision, Mike with his musical intuition now buried under financial practicality, Chloe and David with their creative partnership – they represented different facets of Lukas's life, different paths he might have taken.

But why tonight? And why did Lukas keep touching his pocket with an almost reverent anxiety?

As evening deepened into true dusk, the conversation flowed as freely as the drinks, but undercurrents of tension rippled beneath the surface. Sarah's tales of difficult clients carried an edge of desperation, her laugh a touch too bright when describing her latest design challenges.

"I swear, if Martin tries to take credit for my project one more time, I'll 'accidentally' spill coffee all over his precious golf clubs," she declared, but her eyes held more worry than humour.

Mike's attempts at engagement grew increasingly strained, his smile faltering when he thought no one was looking. During a lull in conversation, Lukas gently pulled him aside, concern etched on his features.

"What's really going on, mate?" he asked softly, lowering his voice beneath the general chatter. "You know you can talk to us, right?"

Mike sighed, his shoulders slumping as if finally releasing a heavy burden. "Sally wants to move in together," he confessed, running a hand through his already dishevelled hair. "And I... I don't know if I'm ready. But if I say no, I think that might be it for us."

"That's a tough spot," Lukas said carefully, studying his friend's troubled face. "Have you talked to her about how you're feeling?"

"I've tried," Mike replied, his voice thick with frustration. "But every time I bring it up, it turns into an argument. I just don't know what to do."

The fairy lights flickered in sympathy, casting strange shadows across their faces. Above them, the first stars were beginning to appear, twinkling faintly through London's ever-present haze. The city's distant hum had taken on an almost physical quality, a background noise for the evening's unfolding drama.

Throughout these conversations, Lukas remained acutely aware of the deck in his pocket. The cards conveyed a vibrating energy against his thigh, not with physical movement but with potential energy—like a vinyl record waiting to be played, needing only the right touch to release its sound into the world.

Each friend's voice triggered specific vibrations from the deck, as if the cards were responding to their presence, recognising the archetypes they unknowingly embodied. The storm clouds now covered the entire sky, the air electric with gathering power.

The moment had come. Lukas felt the weight of the card pack in his pocket grow heavier, more insistent. He extracted the deck with trembling fingers, placing it carefully on the cable drum table. The pack, softened by time and countless touches, caught the dying light.

THE READING

The gold lettering – "FORTUNES TOLD" – conveyed its own inner radiance, each letter dancing with unknowable shadows.

James watched with growing concern, something in his lover's expression triggering an alarm. There was an intensity to Lukas he hadn't seen before – a feverish, almost manic energy that radiated from him in waves. He started to speak, to suggest perhaps they save whatever this was for another time, but the words died in his throat as Lukas opened the pack.

A hush fell over the terrace. The air thickened, charged with a subtle, almost imperceptible energy. Even Sarah, the most sceptical of the group, leaned forward with undisguised curiosity in her eyes. The distant city sounds faded away, leaving them in a bubble of anticipation.

"So," Lukas began, trying to inject a casual tone into his voice despite the tremor in his hands, "These are the cards I found at Portobello. In Cassandra's Emporium." He paused, struggling to find words to describe the inexplicable. "She said… well, she implied they might be special."

"Special how?" Mike asked, his brow furrowed with concern. "Like, going to tell us our futures, special? Are you getting into witchcraft now?"

Lukas laughed nervously, but the sound hung strangely in the air. "Not exactly witchcraft. More like… a tool for self-reflection. Cassandra said they could offer insights, help us see things from a different perspective."

He fanned the cards out across the table in a graceful arc. Each card vibrated with potential, their worn edges catching the fairy lights in unnatural ways. The ancient spires surrounding them appeared to lean in closer, their shadows stretching unfathomably long across the concrete.

James remained silent, watching intently. Normally, he'd have been the first to comment, to analyse, to question. But something held him back – an unfamiliar hesitation born of the strange energy emanating from the cards and from Lukas himself. He'd known Lukas for years, had seen him in every emotional state from ecstatic creativity to the depths of depression when his marketing campaigns were rejected. But this was something new – a Lukas he didn't recognise, driven by something he couldn't name.

Sarah, ever the pragmatist, volunteered to go first. "Right," she said, her voice regaining its usual assertiveness, though something flickered behind her eyes. "Enough with the mystique. Let's see what these mysterious cards have to say."

As Sarah reached for a card, the atmosphere around them shifted subtly. The fairy lights dimmed slightly, as if holding their breath. The air around her fingers thickened, creating a visible resistance that made Sarah hesitate momentarily. When her fingertips finally contacted the card, a tiny static spark jumped between them—visible to everyone around the table.

Justice emerged from the deck. As Sarah lifted it, a gust of wind moved across the terrace, rattling the potted herbs. Overhead, clouds began to gather at an unnatural speed, their edges tinged with a strange purplish light.

"Justice," Lukas explained, watching as Sarah's carefully maintained facade cracked slightly. "It speaks of truth, fairness, cause and effect—the universal law that our actions have consequences. A time of reckoning or decision where balance must be restored."

Sarah's fingers traced the card's edge, her professional demeanour wavering. The images on the card appeared to shift and flow, becoming more pronounced as she stared. In the distance, a church bell began to toll, though none of them could recall a church close enough to be heard so clearly.

"Well," she said, her voice unusually quiet, "I suppose we all have to face the music eventually, don't we? Even when we think we've gotten away with something." Her words carried a hint of humour, but behind them lurked the memory of that speeding ticket she'd stuffed in her glove compartment three weeks ago, her pristinely maintained reputation as a model citizen suddenly seeming a little less immaculate.

A low rumble of thunder punctuated her words, though the storm still appeared distant. James cast a concerned glance skyward, frowning at the rapidly gathering clouds that hadn't been in any forecast.

Mike drew next, his hand trembling more visibly as he approached the deck. The fairy lights above him began to flicker in rhythm with his heartbeat, casting unnatural shadows across the terrace. The city sounds below faded further, replaced by a low, barely audible humming. As his fingers brushed against the cards, the temperature around them dropped perceptibly, breath turning to misty vapour in the suddenly chilled air.

His card was The Fool. The figure on the card teetered on the cliff edge, though there was no breeze. The card radiated an energy that made his fingers tingle and the image gave the impression of breathing, the youthful wanderer's chest rising and falling in perfect synchronisation with Mike's own troubled breaths. Around them, the plants began to sway in unnatural rhythms, their movements resembling the carefree, upward stance of The Fool, reaching toward possibility. "The Fool," Lukas said, watching his friend's internal struggle play out across his features. "It represents new beginnings, innocence, taking a leap of faith. Sometimes a need to embrace uncertainty and step into the unknown to move forward."

Mike visibly paled, his usual joviality completely stripped away. "Well, that's... convenient," he laughed nervously, rubbing the back of his neck. "A leap into the unknown is exactly what I've been avoiding". The card pulsed in his hands, the suspended figure's expression shifting between peace and struggle.

The humming grew louder, and several glasses on the table began to vibrate, inching toward the edge without anyone touching them. The thunder sounded again, closer now, and a flash of lightning illuminated the gathering clouds. The light it cast appeared wrong somehow—too blue, too lingering, revealing shapes in the clouds that defied explanation.

Chloe and David drew together, their hands intertwined as they selected their cards. As they reached toward the deck, the fairy lights surged brightly, then dimmed almost to darkness before flaring back to life. The shadows cast by their movements appeared to lag behind by fractions of a second, creating visual echoes across the terrace. The potted herbs released their scents with sudden intensity, the fragrances twisting together into something ancient and unfamiliar.

The Lovers appeared for David, while The Ace of Cups emerged for Chloe. Where their cards touched on the table, the air conveyed a shimmering quality, creating a small distortion in the space between them. Their combined energy was palpable, making the fairy lights flutter and dance wildly. The images on both cards were clearly moving now, the figures turning to look directly at the couple with eyes that held infinite knowledge.

"These cards…" Chloe whispered, her eyes wide with wonder. "They feel…"

"Alive," David finished, his usual pragmatism giving way to awe.

Lightning flashed again, followed almost instantly by a crack of thunder that made them all jump. The storm was directly overhead now, though not a drop of rain had fallen. The thunderclap summoned a sudden, violent gust of wind that swept across the terrace, scattering the remaining deck. A single card broke free from the pile, sliding across the table with unnatural purpose before coming to rest directly before James. It turned itself over with deliberate slowness, revealing The Magician—its figure standing tall with one arm raised toward heaven, eyes boring into James with unsettling recognition.

James recoiled, his breath catching. "I—I didn't choose that."

"It chose you," Lukas murmured.

"No." James shook his head vehemently, a cold sweat breaking across his forehead. "I'm not playing this game any more." With a sharp, decisive motion, he swiped at The Magician, sending it skittering back toward the scattered pile. The group fell silent, the air suddenly thick with tension. For three heartbeats, nothing happened. Then, as if repelled by an unseen force, the card immediately reversed its trajectory—sliding back across the surface with deliberate purpose. It stopped precisely where it had been before, directly in front of James, only now the figure in the illustration wore what could only be described as a smile. James's face drained of colour as he pressed back against his chair, the wood creaking in protest. "Did you see that?" he whispered, his usual strong front crumbling before their eyes.

As their cards settled on the table, the terrace floor beneath the Persian rug began to vibrate gently. The city beyond their sanctuary started to blur at its edges, buildings and streets melting into one another like watercolours in rain. The boundaries between objects—so firm and certain moments before—now gave the impression of negotiability, fluidity.

By now, no one could deny something extraordinary was happening. The air had grown heavy with potential, each breath drawing in more than oxygen—drawing in possibility itself. The cards left on the table had begun to arrange themselves in motifs without being touched, edges tapping against the wood in a rhythm that sounded like ancient code.

James reached for Lukas more forcefully now, his scientific mind struggling to process what his senses were telling him. "This isn't right," he said, voice tight with alarm. "We should stop."

But one card remained stubbornly face down on the table, resisting all attempts to ignore it. It conveyed its own heartbeat, a living thing waiting to be acknowledged.

With trembling hands, Lukas turned over the final card.

The Tower.

The image on the card writhed and transformed before their eyes, no longer a flat illustration but a three-dimensional scene unfolding in miniature. The tower itself rose from the card's surface, its stone walls weathered and ancient. Lightning struck its pinnacle repeatedly, each flash illuminating the terrified figures tumbling from the heights. Their silent screams conveyed audibility somehow, a high-pitched keening at the edge of perception.

The card radiated an energy that was almost painful to touch, a promise of destruction and unavoidable change. Lukas couldn't release it, his fingers fused to its surface. The Tower's destruction played out in an endless loop, collapse and restoration, collapse and restoration, with each cycle the figures falling differently, showing infinite possible outcomes.

"Lukas," James said, his voice barely audible above the storm that had materialised from nowhere, "what have you done?"

The first rumble of thunder was so deep it vibrated through their bones, not a sound but a physical force that rattled their teeth and blurred their vision. Storm clouds gathered with unnatural speed, roiling and churning like a living entity aware of its purpose. Lightning illuminated the clouds from within, revealing shapes that defied explanation—spiral staircases leading nowhere, doors opening onto void, faces forming and dissolving in the vapour.

Reality began to fray around them. The comfortable terrace furniture warped and twisted, wood grain flowing like water, metal bending like soft wax. The fairy lights exploded one by one in showers of multi-coloured sparks, each burst accompanied by a sound like distant bells or breaking glass.

The potted herbs bent and swayed in arrangements that had nothing to do with the wind, their leaves spelling out words in ancient alphabets before dissolving into new shapes. The Persian rug rippled beneath their feet, its motifs swirling hypnotically, revealing hidden designs that conveyed mapping unknown territories.

"This isn't natural," Sarah whispered, her voice barely audible above the storm. "Lukas, what's going on?"

The cable drum table began to vibrate, its surface rippling like water. The remaining cards danced across its surface of their own accord, arranging and rearranging themselves in complex configurations. Each arrangement conveyed a different story, revealed a different possible future.

Mike stumbled backward, his face ashen. "The buildings," he gasped, pointing toward the city skyline. "Look at the buildings!"

They all turned to see London transforming before their eyes. The familiar architecture was twisting, stretching, becoming something else entirely. Modern glass towers bent like reeds in the wind, their reflective surfaces showing unthinkable angles. The Victorian buildings appeared to breathe, their brickwork flowing like liquid, windows becoming eyes that blinked and watched with ancient intelligence.

The Thames itself was visible now despite the distance, its waters running backward, glowing with an internal phosphorescence that traced arrangements across its surface. The moon hung too large and too close in a purple sky, its cratered surface clearly visible, craters that formed faces that turned to watch the terrace.

Chloe clutched David's hand tighter, their fingers white-knuckled. "We need to get inside," she said, her voice shaking. "Now!"

A bolt of lightning split the sky directly overhead, its thunder immediate and deafening. The air itself cracked, revealing glimpses of another London behind it—a city of unfathomable architecture and ancient magic, where the Thames flowed backward and the moon hung too large and too close in a purple sky.

"Inside!" Lukas shouted, snatching up The Tower card. Its surface burned against his hand, but he couldn't let it go. "Everyone inside!"

They scrambled for the door, abandoning glasses and plates as the storm's fury increased. The Persian rug came alive beneath their feet, its motifs swirling and shifting, threatening to tangle their legs. The mismatched chairs clattered against each other like wind chimes made of bone and wood, their shadows stretching beyond natural explanation in the strange light.

The cards pulsed with their own heartbeat as Lukas clutched them to his chest. Each one radiated heat through his shirt, burning with individual intensity. The Tower card in particular seared against his hand, its energy wild and untamed.

The metal door to the stairwell felt ice-cold against their hands, its surface crawling with tiny fractal arrangements of frost despite the summer evening. As they tumbled through the doorway, it slammed behind them with the finality of a tomb being sealed. The sound echoed through the stairwell like a bell tolling midnight in an empty church.

4

A Storm Breaks

The storm raged outside, but there was nothing natural about its fury. Lightning forked across the sky in impossible patterns, briefly illuminating clouds that churned like living things. The wind didn't just howl – it seemed to speak, carrying whispers in languages that had never graced human tongues.

In the sudden quiet of the enclosed space, they stood breathing heavily, their faces pale in the flickering light, they carefully made their way downstairs. The crystal chandelier above them pulsed erratically, casting strange shadows that didn't quite match their movements. The walls seemed to inhale and exhale gently, like the inside of something alive.

"What..." Sarah started, her voice cracking. She cleared her throat and tried again. "What just happened out there?" Her usual confidence had shattered. Her hands trembled as she clutched her wine glass, the liquid inside rippling in unsettling ways. "That wasn't normal. That wasn't normal at all."

Lukas watched the wine in Sarah's glass. Something about its movement made him deeply uneasy, though he couldn't have explained exactly why. There was a wrongness to it that had nothing to do with physics and everything to do with instinct. The wine wasn't just rippling—it seemed to be moving against the trembling of Sarah's hands, creating patterns that resembled tiny wheels turning within wheels. For a moment, he thought he saw faces forming in the liquid, watching him with ancient eyes. He blinked, and the faces disappeared, but the uneasiness remained.

A particularly vicious gust of wind rattled the windows, making them all jump. The lights flickered wildly, throwing grotesque shadows across the walls. Faces formed in those shadows – ancient, knowing faces that seemed to watch them with detached amusement. They lingered even after the lights steadied, their expressions shifting from curiosity to hunger.

"It's just a storm," David said, his voice carrying a forced calm that fooled no one. "A bad one, sure, but just a storm." Even as he spoke, his words seemed to carry more weight than they should, as if reality itself bent to accommodate them. The air around him briefly solidified, creating a dome-like shimmering that expanded outward before dissipating.

"I don't like this," Chloe whispered, pressing closer to David. "It feels... wrong. Like the air itself is angry." She shivered, though the room wasn't cold. "Can anyone else feel that? Like... like electricity, but alive?"

Lukas nodded, understanding exactly what she meant. The atmosphere was charged, electric, as if the very fabric of reality was stretching and warping around them. He could feel it on his skin, a tingling sensation that raised goosebumps along his arms. The familiar contours of his living room began to shift subtly – corners that should have been right angles seemed slightly off, and the ceiling appeared higher than he remembered.

Looking at his bookshelf, he noticed titles he didn't recognise—or rather, titles that seemed to change as he focused on them. Was that copy of *The Great Gatsby* always bound in green leather with gold symbols embossed on the spine? He could have sworn it was a paperback. The clock on the wall—its numbers weren't in the right order any more and the hands moved irregularly, sometimes forward, sometimes back. These weren't just tricks of the light; something fundamental was changing around them—or perhaps they were changing.

Mike wandered the perimeter of the room, his movements erratic and childlike. Where his fingers trailed along the walls, faint images appeared—fantastical landscapes, strange creatures, doorways opening onto impossible vistas. "It's beautiful," he whispered, "Can't you see how beautiful it all is?"

Sarah moved to examine the wall where Mike had left his mysterious images. "These aren't random," she said, her voice taking on a strange, authoritative quality. "There's a pattern here. A... cycle." She placed her hand on one image—a door standing ajar—and it seemed to solidify under her touch, becoming almost three-dimensional.

Mike sank down against a wall, his knees drawn up to his chest. In the dim light, his face looked different – younger, wilder, with a mischievous cast to his features that hadn't been there before. "The cards," he said softly. "They knew, didn't they? The Fool... that was me. Taking the leap, starting the journey." He laughed, a sound full of wonder and fear.

Chloe was visibly shaking. "Maybe we should call it a night," David suggested gently, but his voice carried an undercurrent of authority that hadn't been there before. The others murmured their agreement, and he began to gather their coats as another clap of thunder shook the building.

"It's those bloody cards," Sarah said suddenly, her voice sharp with accusation. In the subdued light, her face looked different – more animated, with an almost feverish energy, like fortune itself in motion.

When she spoke, her words seemed to spiral through the air, leaving brief after-images like perfectly balanced scales. "Ever since you brought them out, everything's gone mad. Where are they now?"

As Sarah questioned him, Lukas felt a strange sensation—as if she could see all possible futures stretching from this moment, every path his answer might lead them down. Her eyes had taken on a kaleidoscopic quality, seeming to reflect a thousand possible outcomes.

Lukas felt a jolt of panic. His hand brushed against his trouser pocket unconsciously, feeling the warm pulsation of the cards through the fabric. "I... I think I left them outside," he admitted, a wave of guilt washing over him. "I forgot to grab them."

"Good," Sarah said firmly. "Let them blow away. I don't want those things anywhere near us."

But even as she spoke, Lukas felt a pull towards the cards, an inexplicable urge that seemed to connect him to them. He glanced sheepishly at the floor, hoping she wouldn't question him further.

"I'd better be going too," said Sarah. "I have an early client meeting tomorrow." The goodbyes that followed felt heavy with unspoken meaning. Sarah hugged him longer than usual, her embrace carrying a hint of protective fierceness. "Be careful," she whispered, though of what, she didn't specify. As she left, Lukas could have sworn he saw the scales of justice balanced perfectly in her shadow.

Mike chipped in anxiously, "Wait... I'd better be going too. I'll walk you to the station," not really wanting to go out there by himself. "Just to keep you company, you understand," he laughed nervously. Mike's departure was stranger still. He moved with an unusual grace, as if dancing to music only he could hear. At the door, he turned back with an enigmatic smile. "The journey's just beginning, isn't it?" he asked, then disappeared into the storm before Lukas could respond.

As the door closed behind them, James rounded on Lukas. He stepped forward, placing a hand on Lukas's arm. His touch felt electric, charged with an energy that hadn't been there before. "Are you mad?" he asked, his voice tight with fear. "What have you done?"

As James spoke, small sparks danced between his fingers, and the air around his hand seemed to bend light in unusual ways. He didn't appear to notice, but Lukas stared, transfixed by the miniature light show emanating from his friend's skin.

The temperature dropped suddenly, their breath becoming visible in the increasingly frigid air.

"I don't understand what's happening," said Lukas, "it's just a really bad storm." He wondered if James had seen the same things that he had. He felt uneasy, "I just thought... Cassandra said—"

"I don't care what Cassandra said," James interrupted, more angry than Lukas had ever seen him. "I want you to return those cards tomorrow. We'll have no more of this nonsense."

And with that he turned away. Lukas reached for his arm, "I'm sorry... I'll take them back, I promise." James shook it off. "I'm going to bed. We'll tidy up this mess tomorrow." Before Lukas could say anything else, James turned and went upstairs. Lukas called after him, but there was no response. He could hear James moving about angrily, doors slamming, then... silence.

A massive thunderclap shook the building. The windows rattled in their frames as if something was trying to get in. Several panes cracked, forming patterns that looked unsettlingly like staring eyes. The cracks spread with deliberate slowness, creating intricate, jagged patterns across the glass.

Suddenly the French doors flew open, the voile drapes billowing in the breeze like spectral dancers. Books fell from shelves, their pages fluttering open. Lukas ran to close the doors, then bent down to pick up the books. Curiously, one had fallen open on a page that revealed illustrations that Lukas didn't remember – elaborate drawings of strange creatures and impossible landscapes. Where had this come from?

He picked it up, open to a page showing a complex equation written in a slanting, elegant hand. Below it was a signature: Peter Marlowe, 1842. The equation seemed to describe the relationship between two worlds, with variables that made Lukas's head swim. As he stared at it, Lukas thought he could almost understand it—something about parallel realities separated by a permeable membrane of consciousness.

"Something's coming through," Lukas said, the words rising unbidden to his lips. He wasn't sure how he knew, but the certainty filled him like a physical presence. "The cards weren't just cards. They were... doors." And someone had been waiting for those doors to open. Not with malice, Lukas sensed somehow, but with something more complex—a hunger tinged with desperation, a mathematician's obsessive need to understand.

He placed the book back on the shelf, thoughtfully. But doors to what?

He moved towards the doorway and raised his hand to turn off the lights. In the shadows, something stirred. He turned.

The darkness seemed to pulse, thicker than mere absence of light—a living darkness that watched and waited. The scent of ozone and old books hung heavy in the air, overlaid with something sweeter, like overripe fruit.

"Hello, Lukas," came a voice from the shadows. It was pleasant, cultured, with an accent Lukas couldn't quite place—something that suggested both Oxford education and much older origins.

A figure emerged, elegantly dressed in a charcoal suit that seemed to absorb what little light remained. He was handsome in an understated way, with features that appeared both youthful and ancient simultaneously. His eyes, though—his eyes held centuries.

Between his fingers, The Tower card flipped back and forth with casual precision, over and under, a hypnotic motion that seemed impossible given the card had been in Lukas's pocket just moments ago. The card moved with liquid grace, distorting with each turn. The Fool. The Lovers. Justice, The Magician.

"I've been waiting for you," the man said, studying Lukas with an expression that mingled curiosity and amusement. "Not all who find the cards understand their potential. You, however... You have a remarkable talent for transformation."

"Who are you?" Lukas demanded, "How did you get in here?" The stranger smiled—a warm, genuine expression that somehow chilled Lukas to the bone.

"I have many names," he replied, "but you may call me Peter." He extended a hand, the card vanishing from view. "I'm the keeper of the boundaries between worlds. And you, Lukas, have just crossed one."

Lukas stared at the offered hand, noticing how the shadows seemed to cling to it, how the light bent strangely around the fingers. This was no ordinary man—perhaps no man at all.

"Where am I?" Lukas asked, his voice barely a whisper.

Peter's smile widened, revealing teeth that seemed just slightly too perfect. "Welcome to Arcanum," he said, gesturing to the door beside them, "The London between Londons. The city of possibilities."

The door swung open of its own accord, revealing not the hallway but a cobblestone street bathed in purple twilight, lined with buildings that combined Victorian elegance with impossible architecture—doorways that led to nowhere, windows that showed different seasons, chimneys that breathed coloured smoke in patterns that formed words.

"You've been expected," Peter added, his voice now carrying an edge beneath the charm. "The cards always find their way home eventually."

"What do you mean?" Lukas stuttered, suddenly afraid.

"There is nothing to be afraid of," Peter said, his voice carrying an odd resonance that seemed to linger in the air longer than it should. The words themselves felt heavy, weighted with meaning that Lukas couldn't quite grasp. He leaned in close, and Lukas caught a scent that reminded him of old libraries and winter mornings—something both comforting and deeply unsettling. In a voice smooth and deceptively friendly, like honey laced with poison, Peter whispered, "I can give you riches beyond your wildest dreams, show you wonders you won't believe, power you could never contemplate, if you so desire."

The promise hung between them like a living thing. Lukas felt something shift in the air around them, a subtle change in pressure that made his ears pop. The shadows in the room seemed to lean in, as if listening. Even the familiar tick of the wall clock had taken on a different rhythm, slower and more deliberate.

Momentarily, Lukas's curiosity got the better of him. Despite the warning bells chiming softly in the back of his mind, he found himself drawn to the impossible door that had opened beside them—the threshold between his ordinary London flat and the purple-twilight street beyond. He looked towards it, intrigued, his rational mind warring with something deeper, more primal. What was this place? What lay beyond those impossibly architected buildings with their breathing chimneys and season-shifting windows?

Peter saw his hesitation and smiled to himself—an expression of quiet satisfaction, as if watching a chess piece move exactly where he'd predicted it would. There was patience in that smile, the kind that came from having all the time in the world.

"Look around you, Lukas," Peter said, his gesture encompassing not just the room but somehow everything—the cracked windows with their eye-like patterns, the books that had fallen open to pages that shouldn't exist. "You don't need all this." His voice carried a strange authority, as if reality bent slightly to accommodate his words. "This half-life you've been living, these walls that contain nothing but ordinary minutes ticking into ordinary hours."

The observation stung because it was true. Lukas felt the weight of his unemployment, his lack of direction, the way each day seemed to blur into the next without meaning or purpose. Peter's words seemed to reach into his chest and touch something raw and unacknowledged.

"You have no job, no direction, no prospects," Peter continued, his tone gentle but relentless. "But here, in Arcanum, you could be anything. A scholar of impossible mathematics. A navigator of worlds. Someone whose choices actually matter." The card in Peter's hand—now The Magician—caught what little light remained, its surface seeming to pulse with its own inner radiance. "I can change your life... *if* you come with me...."

He held out his hand, and Lukas noticed how the shadows clung to it like living things, how the very air around Peter's fingers seemed to bend and twist in subtle patterns. It was both invitation and test, offering everything and asking for something that Lukas suspected was more precious than he could understand.

For a heartbeat that stretched like an eternity, Lukas almost reached out. The pull was magnetic, irresistible—not Peter himself, but what he represented. Escape. Transformation. The chance to matter in ways that his current existence would never allow.

Then, from somewhere upstairs, came the soft whisper of bedsheets as James shifted in his sleep. The sound cut through Peter's enchantment like a blade through silk, bringing Lukas crashing back to himself.

Lukas suddenly recoiled in horror, the spell broken. The tingling in his fingertips turned cold, almost painful. "No," he said, his voice hoarse with the effort of resistance. "I don't want this." He thought of James asleep upstairs—kind, worried James who had tried to warn him, who had seen the danger long before Lukas had been willing to acknowledge it. His heart ached with the sudden, fierce protectiveness that rose in his chest. "I'm staying here."

Peter's expression shifted, disappointment flickering across his features like a shadow passing over still water. But there was something else there too—a kind of resigned understanding, as if this moment had played out countless times before in countless variations.

"Pity," Peter said, the word carrying layers of meaning that made Lukas's skin crawl. He stepped toward the impossible doorway, his movements fluid and graceful, almost like he was dancing to music only he could hear. At the threshold, he paused and looked back, his eyes holding depths that seemed to stretch back through centuries.

"But our paths are destined to cross again, Lukas. The cards have already shown me as much." His smile was sad rather than threatening, like a parent disappointed by a child's refusal to understand a necessary lesson. "You will change your mind, willingly or unwillingly, and follow. The mathematics of fate are quite precise in this regard."

As the door began to close, sealing away the purple twilight and impossible architecture, Peter's final words drifted back like smoke: "When you're ready to stop pretending that ordinary is enough, you'll know where to find me."

Lukas stood in the darkness, his heart beating loudly in his chest. What had just happened? There was an uneasiness in the pit of his stomach. "James," he thought. He had to talk to James, try to explain.

He gingerly opened the door, not knowing what to expect, but the hallway looked normal. The encaustic tiles did not move, the clock on the wall ticked quietly in a steady rhythm.

Thunder rumbled in the distance, the lightning less frequent now and further away. The storm was subsiding. Everything seemed fine.

Lukas crept upstairs. James was sleeping, looking so peaceful. He breathed a sigh of relief. He wouldn't wake him; he'd make it up to him tomorrow.

As he lay in bed, he could see the moon through a crack in the curtains. It now seemed further away than before. A pool of light shone across the room, but the shadows in one corner gathered more densely than elsewhere. They seemed to form the outline of a tall, slender man.

A STORM BREAKS

For an instant, Lukas thought he could see Peter standing there—not menacing, but observing with intense curiosity, like a scientist monitoring a long-running experiment.

In his hands was what looked like an old leather-bound journal, filled with equations. He smiled sadly at Lukas, then dissolved back into ordinary shadow. Lukas closed his eyes tightly, exhausted by the events of the evening. Tomorrow he would return the cards to the shop as he promised and make up with James. He fell into a fitful sleep.

A shrill, persistent beeping cut through everything. The sound seemed to come from everywhere and nowhere, slicing through the fabric of the moment like a scalpel.

Lukas bolted upright in bed, heart pounding, sheets tangled around his trembling limbs. His alarm clock showed 7:23 AM in glowing red digits, its beeping an assault on the pre-dawn quiet of his bedroom. He slammed his hand down on the snooze button, gasping for breath as if he'd been running.

He looked across at the tangled bedsheets beside him. James wasn't there. He couldn't recall—had James mentioned an early start? He called out: "James... James, are you there?" No reply. Lukas shrugged, trying to dismiss his unease. "Must have left early," he muttered, though something about James's absence felt wrong.

Just a dream? He exhaled shakily, running a hand through his sweat-dampened hair. The cards, the storm, the stranger in the shadows—all just his imagination? The relief was immediate but short-lived.

Something felt wrong. His bedroom looked exactly as it always had—the cluttered bookshelf, the vintage band posters, the clothes draped over a chair—yet everything seemed slightly off-kilter, as if the entire room had been dismantled and reassembled by someone working from a flawed description.

The light coming through the curtains had a purple tinge that didn't belong to any London sunrise he'd ever seen. The air itself tasted different—metallic and sweet, like copper pennies and overripe plums. A subtle vibration hummed beneath his skin, as if reality were a tuning fork struck at the wrong frequency. When he focused on any object for too long, it seemed to shimmer slightly, its edges becoming less certain, and the faintest whisper of unfamiliar music drifted at the edge of his hearing. The alarm clock now read 7:23 AM again, though he was certain several minutes had passed since he'd hit snooze. His fingertips tingled when he touched the bedside table, the wood feeling somehow both solid and insubstantial at once.

"Get it together," he muttered to himself, swinging his legs over the side of the bed. His feet touched the floor, and a jolt of something—not quite electricity, not quite cold—shot up through his body. The sensation lingered as he made his way to the bathroom.

In the mirror, his reflection stared back with an expression he didn't recognise—a split-second delay in movement, as if the reflection were considering whether to follow his lead. When he blinked, he could have sworn his reflection's eyes remained open for a fraction longer than they should have.

The shower felt wrong against his skin—the water pressure fluctuating between too strong and barely there, the temperature shifting unpredictably despite the tap remaining untouched. The steam formed patterns on the glass that dissipated when he tried to focus on them—almost like writing, almost like faces.

Getting dressed, he reached automatically for his favourite shirt, only to find it subtly changed—the fabric slightly different in texture, the buttons aligned on the wrong side. He went down to the living room. No James. He tried his mobile but the message went straight to voicemail.

He tried calling James again, but again no reply. Lukas frowned. Where was he? "Hi James, where are you? I'm really sorry about last night. Call me?"

A STORM BREAKS

Outside his window, London hummed with its usual morning activity, yet the sounds seemed hollow, as if coming from a recording rather than the living city itself. When he looked directly at pedestrians on the street below, they moved with mechanical precision; when glimpsed from the corner of his eye, their movements became fluid, almost dance-like.

He placed the cards in the wooden box. They pulsed and burned uncomfortably against his hand, as if they knew they were going back.

The front door required three attempts before it would lock, the key seeming to reshape itself in his fingers each time he tried to turn it. It was unusually cold, a bitter chill in the air. He noticed that the lime trees were bare. "Odd," he thought, this doesn't feel right somehow. He pulled his coat tighter around him and set out towards Portobello.

At his usual coffee shop, the barista stared a beat too long when he ordered his usual, her smile freezing in place as her eyes widened in what looked unsettlingly like fear.

"You're... you're not supposed to be here," she whispered, then immediately shook her head as if clearing it. "I mean, you're early today. Usually come in after ten, don't you?"

She handed him his coffee with trembling fingers, careful to avoid touching his hand. The other patrons had fallen silent, all eyes on him with expressions ranging from curiosity to alarm. As he left, conversation resumed, but he could have sworn he heard someone say, "How did he get back so quickly?"

On the street, a businessman speaking into his mobile phone stopped mid-sentence as Lukas passed. The man's face drained of colour, and he stepped back against the wall, giving Lukas a wide berth. "Sorry, I'll have to call you back," he said into the phone. "There's... there's something wrong here."

The man's eyes never left Lukas as he continued down the pavement, his gaze burning into Lukas's back long after he'd turned the corner.

The Tower card's image flashed repeatedly in his mind—destruction, transformation, the breaking of foundations. As he moved through the city, he couldn't shake the feeling that he was walking in two worlds simultaneously, his feet in one London while his shadow fell across another.

And in the box he carried, the tarot deck waited, as if alive and breathing—a promise, or perhaps a threat, of something still to come.

5

Familiar Strangers

Lukas found himself standing on cobblestone streets that tilted at subtly unfathomable angles. The world swam back into a semblance of focus, but it was focus filtered through a shattered lens. The air hummed with a low, almost inaudible thrum, vibrating at his perception's edges. Gone was London's gentle grey light; instead, a perpetual twilight bathed everything in shades of amethyst and ochre.

He recognised Covent Garden's distinctive layout, but transformed as if seen through a fun-house mirror. The Royal Opera House's columned façade now spiralled upward in a terrifying gravity-defying helix. The piazza's familiar boundaries had warped, its market hall stretched akin to rubber, cobbled stones arranged in perfect spirals that radiated outward in rhythmic configurations.

"Christ," Lukas whispered, his analytical mind cataloguing the scene as if preparing notes for some last-minute surprise release as he'd done countless times before. "This would make the Turner Prize look positively conventional."

His gaze swept over the transformed landscape. The market stalls, usually vibrant with flowers and trinkets, now overflowed with bizarre, unidentifiable objects. Where one might expect tourist postcards, there were shimmering fabrics that changed configuration with every breath of wind. The familiar artisan cheese shop now displayed crystals that sang in harmonies no human throat could produce, while the former Apple Store housed cages filled with creatures that defied categorisation.

The most unsettling aspect was the people—or rather, the almost-people. They moved with exaggerated grace, their gestures too fluid, expressions too wide, laughter echoing with hollow resonance. Some had skin that shimmered with colours beyond natural explanation, others cast shadows that moved independently and several floated inches above the twisted cobblestones.

A wave of nausea washed over Lukas. He gripped a Victorian lamppost for support, only to find it vibrated beneath his touch, emitting a high, keening note. Unlike the original gas lamps of Covent Garden, this one twisted akin to DNA strands, its light moving with purpose rather than simply illuminating.

"Where am I?" Lukas whispered, his words hanging in the air akin to visible notes.

He gripped the worn box containing the Tarot deck, the only solid, familiar object in this unsettling reality. The questions echoed in his mind, unanswered and terrifying. He needed to find someone, anyone, who could make sense of this madness.

His gaze swept across the distorted square. Then he saw him.

Across the piazza, amidst swirling iridescent bubbles catching strange light akin to liquid rainbows, a figure danced. It was Mike—yet not Mike. The practical accountant with sensible shoes and carefully ironed shirts was gone. This being moved as if his bones had been replaced with quicksilver, limbs bending at angles defying physical explanation and body twisting through shapes that shouldn't have been physically possible.

He wore a patchwork costume seemingly made from pieces of sunset and starlight, bells jingling with every unexplainable leap. A painted grin stretched across his face, colours shifting akin to oil on water. His eyes—oh, his eyes were the most disturbing change. They glittered with unsettling, manic energy, appearing to contain entire universes of chaos and possibility.

Yet Lukas recognised elements of Mike beneath the transformation. The distinctive head-tilt when processing new information. The syncopated rhythm of his movements—Mike had always been the best dancer among them, with an innate understanding of rhythm that made him a natural drummer. Now those qualities were amplified to supernatural proportions, his natural spontaneity unleashed from all constraints. Mike had always been the joker of the group at University, and here that wit and playfulness had exploded into something both magnificent and terrifying.

"Mike?" Lukas called tentatively, taking a hesitant step forward. "Mike, is that you?"

The dancing figure paused mid-pirouette, hanging defying gravity in the air, head cocked at an unnatural angle. The painted grin widened, revealing teeth that seemed just a little too sharp, a little too numerous.

"Mike?" The Fool repeated, his voice a lilting melody that harmonised with itself. "Oh, there's no 'Mike' here, dear traveller. Only the boundless joy of the present moment! The dance of possibility! The... splintering of reality!"

He punctuated each phrase with different unexplainable movements—turning inside out akin to a glove, splitting into multiple copies that danced together before merging back, becoming transparent enough for Lukas to see the twisted buildings through his form before solidifying again.

As Lukas watched, a configuration emerged—not just in the movements, but in the transformation itself. Mike hadn't simply been replaced; he had become an amplified version of himself, human traits exaggerated into something magnificent and terrifying. His natural rhythmic talents now expressed themselves through his entire being, through reality itself.

The Fool hadn't erased Mike but elevated specific aspects of him—his impulsiveness, his wit, his childlike enthusiasm for new experiences—while diminishing others, like his practicality and occasionally dark moods. The transformation followed a logic: core personality aspects amplified, filtered through the archetypal lens of The Fool.

The Fool began circling Lukas, each step leaving flowers that bloomed then withered and died in seconds. As he moved, Lukas noticed something that made his heart clench—a familiar rhythm in The Fool's footfalls, the syncopated arrangement that Mike had always tapped out when thinking, that distinct 5-against-4 poly-rhythm that had become his unconscious signature.

"Mike," Lukas tried again, "if you're still in there... Are the others here too? I need to find James, have you seen him?"

The Fool's eyes flashed with momentary recognition at the names, a flicker of humanity beneath the chaos. But it vanished almost instantly, replaced by renewed manic energy.

"Names, names, so many names!" he sang, performing a backward somersault that defied gravity. "Labels we stick on souls akin to price tags on merchandise! But here in Arcanum, we're more than names, darling. We're archetypes, essences, the distilled truths behind the masks you all wear!"

"Arcanum," Lukas repeated, the word tasting strange yet familiar on his tongue. "Is that where we are?"

"Precisely! Gloriously! Magnificently!" The Fool punctuated each word by transforming—first into a peacock with feathers made of starlight, then a jester juggling miniature planets, then back to his human-ish form. "Arcanum—the hidden realm behind the mundane, the stage behind the curtain, the dream inside the dreamer!"

"What... what happened to the others?" Lukas managed, his voice shaking. "Where's James?" he repeated.

The question appeared to sober The Fool momentarily. His wild movements slowed, and something akin to concern flickered across his painted features. When he spoke again, his voice carried echoes of Mike's normal tones.

"Scattered," he said, gestures suddenly more human. "The storm... the cards... they pulled us all into Arcanum, but not together. They're here, but... transformed. Like me." For a heartbeat, naked fear showed in his eyes—Mike's eyes, not The Fool's—before the chaos rushed back. "But worry not! The paths of Arcanum always cross and cross again! A circle has no beginning, a spiral has no end!"

With that cryptic statement, he spiralled higher into the air. "Follow the cards!" he called down. "They brought you here; they'll guide you through! But beware the Devil—he wears familiar faces and tells such beautiful lies!"

Before Lukas could ask more, The Fool dissolved into a shower of shimmering butterflies that scattered to the winds, carrying fragments of Mike's laughter. Within seconds, he was gone, leaving only a faint echo of bells and the lingering scent of ozone and cinnamon.

Lukas stood alone in the twisted square, the card box a heavy weight in his coat pocket. Arcanum. The name resonated deeply, as if awakening a memory he hadn't known he possessed. The cards had brought him here—perhaps they could indeed guide him. But first, he needed to find his friends, especially James. If they were all transformed akin to Mike, what had they become?

A gentle nudge against his foot startled him from his thoughts. He looked down.

Tonto.

The tortoise was here, miraculously unchanged—solid, real, reassuring. Unlike everything else in this twisted London, Tonto remained constant, his shell bearing the same intricate configurations, his timeless eyes fixed on Lukas with that knowing look he'd had in the shop.

Lukas knelt down, relief washing over him. "Tonto? You're... you're here. How...?"

Tonto, of course, didn't answer. But he nudged Lukas's hand with his head, a surprisingly affectionate gesture. He then turned, deliberately, and began to walk deeper into twisted Arcanum.

As they navigated the distorted streets, Lukas realised Tonto wasn't wandering aimlessly. The tortoise moved with purpose, pausing at intersections to wait for Lukas, adjusting course when dangerous-looking shadows crept too close, guiding them along paths that appeared and disappeared akin to hallucinations.

The air grew thicker, the twilight deeper. They passed distorted landmarks Lukas recognised from his years in London—the British Museum's columned façade now twisting into paradoxical shapes that defied understanding; Trafalgar Square's fountains flowing upward against gravity, Nelson's Column coiled akin to a serpent. Buildings leaned further inward, their facades adorned with gargoyles that appeared to watch with malevolent amusement.

They rounded a corner, and Lukas gasped.

Cassandra's Emporium of Collectible Curiosities stood before him, but no longer the derelict, forgotten shop from Portobello Road. It was... magnificent.

The building soared upwards, defying architecture and physics. Its foundation appeared simultaneously grounded and floating several feet above the cobblestones. Gothic arches melted seamlessly into Art Nouveau curves, which transformed into unfathomably delicate spires that pierced the perpetual twilight sky. Stained glass windows depicted changing scenes with every blink—one moment showing medieval knights battling dragons, the next revealing modern cities dissolving into forests of crystal.

The windows, once grimy and opaque, now glowed with inner light that pulsed akin to a heartbeat. Through them, Lukas glimpsed unfathomable rooms—libraries whose shelves extended into infinity, gardens growing upside down, workshops where objects assembled and disassembled themselves in endless cycles.

As they approached, a section of wall shimmered akin to heat waves, reality folding in on itself to create a doorway. Tonto, without hesitation, walked through.

Lukas followed.

The interior defied comprehension even more than its exterior. Space within appeared to exist in multiple dimensions simultaneously, with rooms that overlapped and intersected in ways that made his eyes water. The air was thick with incense and old paper, overlaid with stranger scents—the metallic tang of lightning, sweet perfume of flowers that had never grown on Earth and the sharp bite of time itself unwinding.

Books bound in materials that shifted under his gaze lined endless shelves. Glowing orbs floated at various heights, each containing what appeared to be miniature worlds. Ancient artefacts hummed with power—swords that sang war songs, mirrors that reflected possible futures and hourglasses filled with what looked suspiciously akin to liquid starlight.

And there, standing amidst this organised chaos, was Cassandra.

She looked exactly as before—her ageless face serene, dark eyes holding knowledge that appeared to span centuries. She wore the same simple, elegant dress, silver hair piled atop her head. Unlike everything else in Arcanum, she remained perfectly, reassuringly constant.

"Welcome, Lukas," she said, her voice a melodious murmur that cut through the ambient sounds. "I've been expecting you."

Lukas felt relief wash over him. Here was someone who might have answers. "Cassandra, I came to bring these back," he said offering up the box, she took the box and placed it on the counter in front of him. "What is this place? What's happening?"

She smiled enigmatically. "This is Arcanum, as your... friend... so eloquently put it. A realm of reflection, of potential, of... transformation." As she spoke, the space around her appeared to ripple, shelves and artefacts responding to her words akin to instruments to a conductor's baton.

"Transformation?" Lukas repeated, glancing back toward the doorway, remembering Mike as The Fool.

"Indeed," Cassandra said, moving through her transformed shop with practised grace. Objects shifted from her path, creating perfect passages through the chaos. "The cards... they have a way of revealing hidden aspects of ourselves, of those around us. They have... awakened something."

"Awakened what?"

"The archetypes," Cassandra said, her gaze drifting toward mirrors reflecting scenes from different times and places. "The fundamental structures of human experience, embodied in the Major Arcana. They are... alive, here. And they have found... hosts."

Lukas felt dread tightening in his stomach. "Hosts? You mean... my friends?"

Cassandra nodded. "They are... reflections. Not quite your friends, not quite the cards. They are... imbued with the energy of the archetypes they drew." She paused, considering carefully. "Each card resonates with different aspects of human nature—The Fool with spontaneity and possibility, Justice with balance and judgment, The Magician with power and transformation. Your friends have become living embodiments of these forces."

"But... why? And why am I still myself?"

Cassandra's expression softened, almost maternal. "Every card found the heart that most aligned with its essence. The Fool found your friend's untapped creativity, his suppressed desire for freedom from structures he built around himself." She moved to a curved window that appeared to look onto dozens of Londons simultaneously. "As for why you remain unchanged... you drew the most powerful card of all—The Tower. Destruction and revelation. The breaking of false structures so truth can emerge."

"I don't understand."

"You are the catalyst, not the transformed. Your role is... different." She moved to a circular table inlaid with moving constellations. "Your journey is one of witnessing, understanding, and ultimately choosing."

"Choosing what?"

"That," Cassandra said with her enigmatic smile, "is for you to discover." She gestured toward Tonto, patiently waiting near a pool of light flowing upward akin to a reverse waterfall. "Tonto will guide you. He knows Arcanum's paths better than anyone."

Lukas looked at the tortoise, his wisdom-filled eyes filled with centuries of wisdom. His presence felt akin to stability in this sea of uncertainty.

"But... I just want to find my friends. I want to go home."

Cassandra's smile held layers of meaning. "Home is not always a place, Lukas. Sometimes, it's a state of being. And sometimes..." she waved her hand, causing air to ripple with configurations of light forming and dissolving akin to soap bubbles, "the journey to find it takes us through unexpected landscapes."

She stepped closer, her touch on his arm surprisingly warm, grounding. "Trust Tonto. Trust yourself. And... be careful. Arcanum holds great wonder, but also great danger. There are forces at play here that you do not yet understand."

"Danger? What kind of danger?"

Cassandra's gaze darkened, lights in the shop dimming in response. "There is one who seeks to control Arcanum, to twist its power. He is... a master of deception, of illusion. He wears many faces, many guises. He is..." she hesitated, air seemingly holding its breath, "the Devil."

The word hung heavy and ominous. The shop grew quieter, as if objects themselves were drawing back in fear.

Before he could speak, a shadow flickered at his vision's edge. It moved akin to smoke but had substance, akin to darkness given form. A figure emerged, materialising from shadows themselves.

It was a man, tall and elegantly dressed in a suit that appeared to absorb surrounding light. His face was handsome, familiar somehow, yet... subtly wrong. There was a cruel twist to his smile, something cold in his eyes that reflected not light, but its absence. The wry, calculated smile was nothing akin to James's warm, genuine expression—this was a perfect, practised curve of lips that never reached those empty eyes.

As the figure approached, Lukas noticed something else—how his movements followed precise mathematical structures, each step calculating exact distances, each gesture solving invisible equations. This precision reminded him painfully of James, whose methodical nature had always been endearing. Yet where James's precision created harmony, this being's exactitude felt akin to a weapon.

"Hello, Lukas," the man said, voice smooth and deceptively friendly. "We meet again, I knew the temptation would be too great... you couldn't resist," he smiled smugly. "Perhaps I can be of some assistance...?"

Lukas knew that voice, though not quite in this form. It carried echoes of James's warm tenor, but distorted, akin to a beloved melody played in a minor key. The man reminded him of the figure that had appeared to him in the living room, Peter, but the face was different. As he came into the light Lukas stepped back aghast.

"James?" he whispered, hope and horror mingling.

The elegant stranger's smile widened, revealing teeth just a touch too perfect. "Peter, actually. Though James is... related to my current manifestation." He adjusted his cufflinks with a gesture painfully familiar—the same precise motion James made before every review of his plans and any changes he'd need to make before his next session. "I am... something more complex. A possibility."

As he spoke, Lukas noticed his hands—long-fingered and graceful, but constantly making small calculations, as if measuring invisible distances or solving equations that existed just beyond normal perception. Once, he caught Peter muttering what sounded akin to a complex algebraic formula under his breath, almost unconsciously.

Tonto showed unprecedented agitation. The tortoise hissed, a low, guttural sound vibrating through the shop's foundations. He shuffled backwards, trying to pull Lukas away by gently butting against his foot. Around them, magical artefacts responded—books slammed shut, mirrors turned away, floating orbs dimmed as if hiding.

Cassandra stepped forward, placing herself between Lukas and Peter. Her presence grew, filling the space with authority that made even the unfathomable architecture bend away. "You know you're not welcome here, Peter," she said firmly, her voice cool but controlled. "You have no dominion here."

Peter chuckled, a sound devoid of warmth that froze the air. "Oh, I think I do, Cassandra." He moved with liquid grace, each step precise and measured. "This realm... it responds to desire, to fear, to... calculation." His eyes never left Lukas. "And there's plenty of that to go around, wouldn't you agree?"

The shadows writhed as he moved, reaching akin to hungry fingers before retreating from Cassandra's steady gaze. Peter's form shifted subtly with each step—sometimes appearing older, sometimes younger, sometimes wearing different faces that Lukas almost recognised.

His gaze locked onto Lukas with hypnotic intensity. "Don't listen to her, Lukas. She wants to keep you trapped in this... illusion." He gestured around at the shop, and for a moment, Lukas saw it flicker, revealing a darker, more seductive version. "I can show you Arcanum's true potential. I can show you... everything."

For a heartbeat, vulnerability flickered across Peter's face—not the confidence of complete control, but something more human. Loneliness? Frustration? It vanished quickly, but not before Lukas noticed.

"And what if I don't want your version of everything?" Lukas asked.

Something genuine flashed in Peter's eyes—surprise, perhaps even respect. "Most people don't know what they want until it's properly quantified," he said, his voice taking on a lecturer's tone. "Reality follows rules, formulae. Even chaos can be predicted with the right equations."

"He's showing you what he thinks you want to see," Cassandra warned. "Peter always does."

"Is it wrong to fulfil desires? To solve problems?" Peter asked, spreading his hands. "I can help you find James—the real James," he said, voice holding something raw and almost yearning. "I can reunite you with all your friends. All I ask is that you consider my perspective."

As he spoke, the air shimmered with possibilities—images of power, knowledge, desires fulfilled. Lukas saw himself wielding unfathomable magic, ruling over vast domains, becoming more than human. The visions were intoxicating, overwhelming.

Lukas felt the pull, a subtle temptation nibbling at his mind's edges. Peter's words painted a seductive picture, and Arcanum, for all its unsettling strangeness, did hold a certain allure.

But there was something hollow behind the promises, something cold behind the familiar features. This wasn't James—it was something wearing fragments of him akin to an ill-fitted mask. James's precision had always served creation and support; Peter's precision felt akin to a weapon.

He looked down at Tonto, whose timeless eyes held a silent plea. Trust me, they appeared to say. The tortoise's steady presence cut through temptation's fog akin to sunlight through storm clouds. As Lukas's gaze lowered, Peter's facade momentarily slipped—his handsome features contorting into a venomous glare of pure malice, only to smooth back into practised charm the instant Lukas looked up again.

"I..." Lukas began, voice shaky but growing firmer, "I don't want what you're offering."

Peter's handsome face transformed instantly, charm cracking to reveal something ancient and terrible beneath. His eyes darkened to bottomless pits, shadows writhing with newfound hunger.

"A pity," he said, voice carrying echoes of countless others, all twisted with malice. "You'll discover that Arcanum has ways of... recalculating... those who resist its truths."

He turned to Cassandra, gaze cold. "You meddle in affairs beyond your computational capacity. The equation is already solved."

For just a moment, as Peter turned away, Lukas caught something in his expression—not confidence, but a flicker of something almost human. Uncertainty? Longing? It vanished quickly, but the impression lingered.

With a final look that promised future encounters, Peter unravelled akin to a thread pulled from a tapestry, taking unnatural shadows with him until only the shop's natural darkness remained.

The tension dissipated, leaving heavy silence. The magical artefacts gradually resumed normal behaviour, though subdued. Lukas felt drained by the encounter. The glimpse of Peter's true nature had been terrifying, a stark reminder of dangers lurking within Arcanum's twisted landscape. Cassandra exhaled slowly, the shop appearing to breathe with her. "He grows stronger. He feeds on doubt, on fear, on... the desire for certainty."

Lukas knelt beside Tonto, gently stroking the tortoise's shell, feeling ancient configurations beneath his fingers. "Thank you," he whispered. "You... you helped me see clearly."

Cassandra nodded. "Tonto has a... keen sense... for deception. He sees beyond surface illusions." She paused thoughtfully. "You were wise to resist. Peter's promises always carry hidden costs."

"I don't understand why he's after me. What does he want?"

"He seeks control," Cassandra said, adjusting bottles containing what looked akin to liquid moonlight. "He aims to reduce Arcanum to calculable variables, to reshape it through cold equations. And you... you represent an unpredictable element in his formulae."

"Me? But I'm just... ordinary."

Cassandra smiled knowingly. "Ordinary is often extraordinary in disguise, Lukas. You possess a strength within—a resilience he cannot calculate. That's why he seeks to corrupt you. Can you help me find my friends?" said Lukas and she smiled "You will need these" she said and took the pack of cards from the box, "You were always meant to have these, you were chosen for a reason" and handed them to him. They pulsed akin to a heartbeat in his hand. Lukas pushed them into his pocket, if he needed them to find his friends, then it would have to be.

She gestured toward the shimmering light-pool where Tonto waited. "The journey ahead will be difficult. You will face trials, temptations, betrayals. But you must not lose hope. You must find courage to embrace your true self, to discover the magic within you. Only then can you hope to overcome the darkness threatening Arcanum... and perhaps, find your way home."

Lukas looked at Tonto, timeless eyes reflecting swirling light. He felt determination surging, a flicker of hope amidst fear. Finding James would be next, wherever and whatever he had become... and Sarah —Justice, with her strong moral compass amplified into cosmic judgment. He had to fight, not just for himself, but for his friends, for Arcanum, and for the chance to return to the world he knew—changed, perhaps, but still himself.

He took a deep breath, squared his shoulders, and with Tonto by his side, stepped toward the unknown.

6

The Magician's Trap

The descent felt less akin to stairs and more akin to a slide into a dream. Each step shifted beneath their feet, the staircase pulling them downward with gentle insistence. The air thickened with each turn, carrying a scent that prickled Lukas's nose – ozone, burnt sugar, and something indefinably old.

Lukas glanced down at Tonto, concerned about the tortoise navigating the strange staircase. He bent down and gently lifted him up, tucking the tortoise securely under his arm - the shell gleaming in the dim light as they made their way down the passageways together. Lukas felt oddly comforted by the familiar weight of his companion as they descended towards the rooms below, the tortoise's presence grounding him amidst growing visual chaos. From below, delicate flashes mingled with shadows and pulses of light that danced across his vision. What first appeared akin to chaos gradually revealed itself to his trained eye as something hauntingly beautiful.

"I know this place," Lukas murmured, though he couldn't possibly have been here before. "There's a club further on... evocative of that speakeasy in Soho you almost always never manage to find when you're looking for it"

As they descended deeper into the darkness, the walls shimmered with phosphorescent configurations that shifted when he tried to focus on them.

At last, they reached the club. A swirling vortex of colour and shapes. Walls undulated akin to liquid, occasionally solidifying into brief, recognisable forms before melting back into kaleidoscopic flow. The ceiling shimmered akin to a heat haze, offering glimpses of constellations from no earthly sky.

Despite the apparent chaos, Lukas felt a strange familiarity. There was an order to it, a hidden logic that reminded him powerfully of James – the way he would bring structure to creative chaos, finding configurations where others saw only randomness. This place felt akin to James's mind turned inside out, his architectural precision applied to the fabric of reality.

Patrons drifted through the space akin to ethereal spectres, their laughter crystallising in the air as delicate structures. On a stage that existed in multiple locations simultaneously, performers created visual spectacles that constantly transformed, creating imagery freed from all constraints.

"James?" Lukas called out, his voice feeling thin and reedy against the ambient hum.

A figure detached itself from a vortex of emerald and violet light, resolving into what appeared to be James. But something felt wrong, akin to looking at a portrait painted by someone who had studied photographs without meeting the subject. The figure wore James's face with unsettling precision, yet there was an artifice to it. This 'James' was clad in costume woven from captured moonlight and solidified shadows. His skin had taken on an otherworldly sheen, and his eyes held the depth of infinite space but lacked the warm authenticity that had always characterised the real James's gaze.

The impersonation was masterful—capturing James's methodical precision and unwavering attention to detail with studied accuracy. The way he moved his hands mimicked James's practised confidence, and the tilt of his head when he concentrated was a perfect recreation. But occasionally, there was a microscopic hesitation before certain gestures, as if recalling a rehearsed movement rather than acting from natural habit.

Lukas recognised the careful movements the figure used—nearly identical to how James had always arranged his marketing campaigns – the deliberate precision, the meticulous attention to every detail of an image. But now those movements warped reality, those careful fingers reshaping the world rather than photographs.

"Lukas! My darling, you've finally come to me!" The Magician's voice was James's, but enhanced with a resonance that made Lukas's heart ache. Golden sparks erupted from his fingertips, forming intricate configurations that danced between them.

"James..." Lukas began, but The Magician raised a finger to his lips, the gesture achingly familiar.

"I remember who I was," The Magician said with studied tenderness. "Just as I remember every moment we shared." He waved his hand, and the air between them shimmered into a living canvas of memories – their first meeting in the university courtyard where James had approached him with insightful comments about lighting techniques; quiet evenings spent examining marketing layouts while Lukas nestled against his shoulder; their first kiss in the rain outside that jazz club in Soho.

Each memory looked perfect but felt hollow, akin to film sets constructed from someone else's detailed notes rather than lived experiences. The Magician hadn't just recreated these scenes; he'd researched them with meticulous care.

"James... what's happened to you?" Lukas whispered, reaching out toward the shimmering figure.

The Magician smiled. "Evolution, darling. I've become what I was always meant to be. The limitations are gone – all those frustrating barriers between imagination and creation. Don't you see? This is freedom."

He began to move his hands through the air with James's characteristic precision. The air itself responded to his touch, becoming a medium as malleable as the materials James had once drafted with such care.

"Remember that night in your flat," The Magician said, his voice dropping to an intimate whisper, "when I stayed up until dawn, redesigning your studio space after you felt it wasn't working for your photography?"

As he spoke, the air rippled, and Lukas saw the scene materialise – James hunched over his drafting table, surrounded by empty tea cups, painstakingly reimagining the space to better serve Lukas's creative process. It had been an act of love that moved Lukas to tears.

"I could see what you couldn't," The Magician continued, his eyes gleaming with passion, though occasionally flickering with calculation that had never been present in James's gaze. "The structures beneath the surface, the architecture behind the art. But I was so... limited then." He flicked his wrist – an almost-perfect reproduction of James's gesture when indicating a design element – and the scene transformed. Now James stood amid floating architectural elements that he manipulated physically. "Now I can create directly, without tools or technology between my vision and reality."

A deck of cards appeared in his hands – the same deck James had carried everywhere during university. As The Magician's fingers danced over them, the cards morphed into iridescent butterflies bearing familiar faces – Sarah, Mike, Chloe and David. Most disturbing was the butterfly bearing Lukas's own face, its wings beating in perfect rhythm with his heart.

"Remember our university days?" The Magician asked with seemingly genuine fondness. "Those late nights when you'd put aside your camera to watch me practice card tricks? You'd lie on that terrible sofa, half-asleep, saying you were paying attention..."

Lukas did remember. Those quiet evenings when James would practice sleight of hand for hours, his face a mask of concentration. Even then, there had been something mesmerising about watching those careful hands create illusions. But that had been harmless misdirection that ended with laughter and kisses. This was something else entirely.

Lukas found himself unable to move, torn between yearning and fear. Tonto pressed closer to his foot, the tortoise's solid presence a reminder of something important.

"That campaign." The Magician said suddenly, his voice gentling. "You know. The one that should have been your masterpiece." His words touched the exact wound that had been festering in Lukas's heart for years. "I can make it real for you now. Not just images, but actual physical spaces – architecture that flows between worlds, visuals that live and breathe."

He gestured, and the floor transformed into structures defying natural explanation. Transparent staircases spiralled upward, rooms unfolded akin to origami, and archways led to vistas that couldn't possibly exist within the confines of this space. The structures displayed images as light flowed through them – a hauntingly familiar visual from one of Lukas's unfinished works, now realised with all the complexity he'd envisioned.

Tears sprang to Lukas's eyes as he witnessed his true vision finally realised – the interweaving themes, the subtle shifts, the complex arrangements that executives had deemed "too challenging." It was beautiful, perfect, exactly what he'd imagined.

"That's what you've always wanted, isn't it?" The Magician continued gently. "To create without limitation. To make images that transform not just emotions but reality itself."

Each word struck Lukas with painful accuracy. How many times had he sat frustrated at his laptop, knowing the vision in his head was beyond the capabilities of the software to realise?

"I can give you that power now," The Magician promised, his eyes shining with what appeared akin to genuine love. "We can create together again, Lukas – but this time with no barriers between your imagination and reality."

Tonto shifted against Lukas's ankle, the movement breaking his trance momentarily. The tortoise's timeless eyes looked up at him with quiet wisdom.

"Come closer," The Magician beckoned, extending his hand – that same hand that had once held Lukas's during their darkest moments. The air around his fingers shimmered and distorted, reality folding in on itself.

As The Magician's hand extended toward him, memories flickered through Lukas's mind – late-night conversations, shared laughter, quiet moments of connection. But something felt wrong. The memories appeared to shift subtly, emphasising moments when James had guided him, directed him, shaped his choices. The alterations were delicate – not crude falsifications but gentle re-framings.

Tonto moved slightly, his shell bumping against Lukas's foot. In that moment of clarity, Lukas saw what was happening – The Magician was remixing their shared history, creating a narrative where Lukas had always needed James's guidance to succeed.

As Lukas hesitated, The Magician's face flickered with momentary impatience. "Still so cautious, Lukas, even here?" he chided. "Always holding back, afraid to fully commit to your vision. It's why they demanded those changes to your marketing campaign, isn't it? Not lack of talent, but lack of... conviction."

The words struck deep, precisely targeting Lukas's greatest creative insecurity. Yet in their cruelty, they revealed something important – this wasn't James at all. The features might be James's, the voice a perfect imitation, but beneath the illusion lurked Peter's manipulative cruelty. The real James would never have weaponised that wound.

"You're not James," Lukas said, his voice stronger than expected. "Peter. This is your trap, isn't it? The James I love used his precision to build, to support, to elevate others. Not to manipulate and display power akin to what you're doing now."

Tonto pressed firmly against his ankle, amplifying Lukas's resolve. The Magician's smile widened, revealing teeth that appeared just a little too sharp. For an instant, something alien flashed in his eyes – something cold and hungry that had never existed in James's warm gaze.

"Oh, but it could be him, Lukas. Don't you want James back? Wouldn't you do anything to recover what was lost?" The disguise held, but the voice had shifted subtly, revealing hints of Peter's cadence beneath the perfect mimicry.

He gestured with elegant precision, and their surroundings transformed into their old university common room. But this version was wrong – the walls breathed in slow rhythm, the furniture writhed with suppressed life, and through the windows, geometries twisting against comprehension twisted against a sky that burned with cold fire.

"Now I can reshape reality according to our desires," The Magician said warmly. "Think of what we could create together – not just photographs, but entire worlds."

Tonto nudged against his foot, a steady presence. Lukas bent down, the tortoise's shell felt oddly warm to the touch, a small anchor in a world rapidly unravelling.

"I know James," Lukas said steadily, "The real James. He didn't need magical powers to create beauty. And he would never use my insecurities against me akin to what you're doing now, Peter."

Something flickered across The Magician's face – a momentary crack in the perfect disguise, a glimpse of frustration beneath the performance. But then his smile widened again, revealing that predatory gleam.

"Those memories are real," The Magician acknowledged. "But they're only fragments of a story that's still unfolding. I can be everything you need – creator, muse, partner, guardian – with powers beyond anything either of you dreamed possible."

He snapped his fingers, and the space fractured into floating mirrors. Each showed not reflections, but visions of possible futures that pulled at Lukas's heart.

In one, Lukas saw himself alone at his desk, his face etched with loneliness as he sipped tea, surrounded by half-finished photographic proofs. In another, Lukas stood before architectural structures defying comprehension that displayed his images as light flowed through them, transforming viewers into something more than human.

Tonto moved silently between Lukas and the most seductive mirror. The tortoise didn't block the view, but his presence provided a counterpoint to the overwhelming temptation.

Lukas found his gaze drawn to one mirror slightly apart from the others. Unlike the rest, it showed a simple scene – himself at his light table, James sitting nearby with architectural plans, both working in companionable silence. There was no spectacular magic, just quiet intimacy. That image made Lukas's heart ache with profound longing.

As Lukas stared at that simple reflection, he realised it contained something the magnificent visions lacked – a genuine connection, an equality of presence. This wasn't about power but authentic connection, something Peter's temptations couldn't truly provide.

As Lukas wavered, Tonto butted his foot sharply. The contact grounded Lukas, clearing his vision. For a heart-stopping moment, he saw beyond the facade to the truth beneath – Peter's desperate hunger behind The Magician's eyes, a void that threatened to consume everything.

"No," Lukas said firmly. "You're wearing James akin to a costume, Peter. But you're not him. You never will be."

The Magician's expression cracked. For an instant, what looked out from those eyes was Peter, frustrated that his elaborate trap had failed. Then the charm vanished, replaced by chilling coldness.

"How... perceptive," he hissed. "But seeing the trap doesn't mean you can escape it."

The mirrors closed in, forming a cage. Each showed a different vision – some seductive, others terrifying. The visions were arranged with calculated precision to create maximum emotional impact.

In desperation, Lukas reached for the card deck in his pocket. His fingers closed around The Tower card, which appeared to burn with cold fire. He held it up akin to a shield, driven by pure instinct.

The effect was immediate. The card blazed with brilliant light, sending shock waves that cracked the mirrors. The Magician recoiled, his magnificent costume suddenly tattered at the edges, revealing glimpses of ordinary clothing beneath.

"No!" The Magician howled, but suddenly his expression changed dramatically. The performance shifted into an even more cunning manipulation as he adopted a perfect impression of a desperate James.

"Lukas?" he gasped, reaching out with the same gentle movement James had always used when offering comfort. "What's happening to me? I'm trapped in here—"

The performance was heartbreaking in its accuracy. For a moment, Lukas almost believed it was really James fighting to surface from within some magical prison. He reached toward the outstretched hand instinctively, their fingertips almost touching.

Then he saw it – a fleeting expression of calculated satisfaction that

Peter couldn't quite hide. This wasn't James trapped; it was Peter playing his cruellest trick yet.

Tonto nudged Lukas toward a sliver of space between two mirrors – a tiny gap in the seemingly impenetrable wall. Heart pounding, Lukas scooped up Tonto.

"I'll find the real James," he whispered. "Not your illusion."

Then he ran, squeezing through the narrow opening. Behind him, The Magician's laughter echoed – a sound that began as mockery but transformed into frustrated rage as the disguise slipped further.

They fled through spaces that defied reality, corridors that twisted back on themselves, rooms where up became down. Each chamber revealed new geometries defying explanation, yet even in his panic, Lukas recognised how Peter had studied James's architectural style to craft this elaborate trap – a methodical approach to madness that mimicked his lover's mind with disturbing precision.

Finally, they burst through a door into what appeared to be a London alleyway, though distorted into something alien. The cobblestones writhed beneath their feet, and buildings leaned at angles beyond natural explanation, their windows watching akin to hungry eyes.

From the depths of the club, The Magician's voice echoed, "This isn't the end, Lukas. Arcanum is a web, and I am at its centre. Every path leads back to me."

The threat carried an undercurrent of frustration that confirmed Lukas's suspicion. This trap had been meticulously planned, Peter's attempt to capture him through his love for James.

The alleyway stretched before them, a labyrinth of shadows and distorted perspectives. Buildings twisted at angles defying comprehension, windows reflecting the unnatural glow of gas lamps burning with cold fire.

"Thank you," Lukas whispered to Tonto. The tortoise blinked up at him with eyes that held centuries of wisdom. Then Tonto turned and began to move forward with deliberate purpose, as if following an invisible path through the chaos.

As they made their way deeper into the twisted version of London, Lukas felt a strange mixture of grief and determination. He would find the real James, not the illusion Peter had crafted to trap him. But first, he needed to understand this world – and for that, he would follow the ancient tortoise who had already saved him from the first great temptation of Arcanum.

7

Court of Revelations

The familiar spires of Westminster transformed before Lukas's eyes, reality warping like heated glass. Gothic arches stretched and twisted, defying not just architecture but fundamental perception itself. Flying buttresses curled like serpents, their stone surfaces rippling with unfathomable fluidity. Where orderly towers had once stood as symbols of democratic stability, now rose a cathedral of chaos, its spires puncturing a sky the colour of fresh bruises.

The distortions weren't random but meaningful—as if Westminster had always contained this second form, visible only from a particular angle of consciousness. Each transformed element revealed something of its essential nature rather than merely changing shape. It was less destruction than revelation—the same building viewed through a different lens of awareness, its hidden meanings suddenly laid bare.

The building breathed, its walls expanding and contracting with slow, deliberate movements. Stained glass windows depicted scenes that shifted and changed with each passing moment – one instant showing familiar biblical scenes, the next offering clear views of cosmic truths that made Lukas's eyes water. Gargoyles peered down with faces he recognised: his local barista, his former instructor, the woman who walked her poodle past his house every morning.

These shifting scenes weren't chaotic but suggestive, akin to dream imagery expressing deeper meanings beneath their surface appearances. The gargoyles' familiar faces—disturbing in their recognition—seemed to imply that everyone contained multitudes, archetypes hidden beneath everyday identities. Ordinary people bearing extraordinary significance, waiting only for the right perspective to reveal their true nature.

The early morning sun's light spilled behind the transformed cathedral, but instead of the gradual brightening of an ordinary sunrise, light spilled forth in distinct rays, as if the sun were a conscious entity deliberately choosing where to illuminate. Each beam struck the twisted architecture at precise angles, creating shadows that formed intricate configurations across the courtyard where Lukas stood – configurations reminiscent of forgotten languages when viewed with unfocused eyes.

The light revealed rather than merely illuminated, showing not just what was there but what had always been there, unseen. Every shadow cast meaning rather than mere absence; every highlight emphasised truth rather than mere presence. Light itself seemed conscious, intentional—revealing the cathedral's dual nature as both physical structure and metaphysical statement.

Tonto moved differently here. The venerable tortoise's usual methodical pace took on a ceremonial quality, each step placed with deliberate reverence. His shell caught the strange light, reflecting it in ways that created miniature auroras around his form. He led Lukas toward an entrance that constantly shifted – sometimes a modest doorway, sometimes a towering archway, occasionally dissolving entirely into a shimmering curtain of light before reforming.

Lukas's heart hammered against his ribs as vertigo washed over him.

This wasn't just architectural distortion; it was reality itself coming undone at the seams. Beside him, Tonto remained blessedly unchanged, his timeless shell gleaming faintly in the strange, purplish light that seemed to emanate from the very stones of the building.

"I suppose we go in?" Lukas mumbled, his voice barely a whisper. He felt an absurd urge to knock, as if this were a perfectly ordinary social call. Tonto responded by butting his ankle with surprising force, propelling him forward.

The enormous doors – carved with scenes that moved when viewed from the corner of his eye – swung inward with theatrical grace. The interior defied all possibility. The Great Hall stretched far beyond what the building's exterior should have contained, its marble columns spiralling upward into infinite darkness. Each column bore carved faces that tracked Lukas's movement – he recognised his neighbour he only ever spoke to at the dry cleaner's, Mr. Abernathy from the bookshop, colleagues from his former office. Though frozen in stone, each face held an unsettling awareness.

The unfathomable dimensions weren't arbitrary magic but manifestations of deeper truth—the hall's vastness representing not spatial impossibility but the limitless nature of consciousness itself. The watching faces weren't random decorations but reminders that perception is always bidirectional—that to see is also to be seen, to recognise is to be recognised. The cathedral wasn't merely larger inside; it was revealing the true dimensions that ordinary perception habitually compressed.

"Welcome, Seeker," boomed a voice that resonated with the force of a cathedral organ. Lukas spun around, his hand reaching instinctively for a weapon he didn't possess.

Before him stood Mr. Richards from number 47 – yet not Mr. Richards at all. Gone was the befuddled retired professor who handed out peppermints and tended prize-winning begonias. In his place stood The Emperor, radiating power that made the air crackle with static electricity. His tweed jacket had transformed into flowing robes that shifted between deep indigo and regal purple, embroidered with constellations that actually twinkled. His thinning silver hair had become a crown of living starlight, and his once-watery blue eyes now held the weight of centuries.

"Mr. Richards?" Lukas's voice sounded small in the vast space.

"That name holds no meaning here," The Emperor replied, each word carrying the gravity of law. "You stand in the Court of Revelations, where truth strips away all masks."

From the swirling shadows emerged two more figures. Mrs. Chen from the corner shop had transformed into The Hierophant, her ceremonial robes of deep crimson and gold replacing her usual cheerful florals. Venerable symbols writhed across the fabric like living things, each one trying to whisper secrets directly into Lukas's mind.

Behind her glided Sarah. "Sarah?" said Lukas. "Sarah, it's me Lukas." Her head turned to face him, but her eyes were dark and soulless, she looked straight through him, there was no flicker of recognition, she did not reply. Though he recognised her immediately—the same petite figure with short blonde hair he knew as a sharp businesswoman in pin-stripe suits in London—this was Sarah embodying Justice. Clothed now in robes of pure white and shimmering gold, her authoritative posture and commanding presence remained intact— essential characteristics of her true nature now revealed rather than transformed. This wasn't a physical metamorphosis but a revelation of her inner strength and balance made manifest. A sword of solidified moonlight hung at her hip, its edge radiating cold certainty.

"We have awaited your arrival," The Hierophant said, her voice carrying echoes of forgotten prophecies. "Though few cross the veil by choice, fewer still find their way to this sanctuary."

Each Arcana figure embodied concepts rather than mere alterations—

The Emperor standing not just for power but the eternal principle of order itself; The Hierophant representing not religion but the bridge between material understanding and spiritual insight; Justice manifesting not law but the fundamental balance underlying all existence. They weren't simply transformed humans but human forms shaped by eternal principles, showing how archetypes exist within ordinary people, waiting to be recognised.

Lukas stepped forward, willing himself to stand straighter despite his exhaustion. "I didn't exactly cross by choice. I'm trying to find my friends – to understand what's happening."

The Emperor raised an eyebrow, the gesture reminiscent of how Mr. Richards used to react to neighbourhood gossip. "And yet you brought the cards. You drew The Tower." His voice deepened, reverberating through the vast chamber. "Some choices are made before we are conscious of making them."

Justice moved forward, her steps leaving ripples in the air akin to stones dropped in still water. "You seek answers, Lukas. But are you prepared for the weight of truth? Can you bear the responsibility of knowledge?"

Tonto shuffled forward, positioning himself protectively between Lukas and the assembled Arcana. The tortoise's presence seemed to alter the energy in the hall, making the shadows retreat slightly. The Emperor's expression softened, though power still radiated from him in palpable waves.

"The beast of ages vouches for you," he declared, his voice setting the very stones humming. "That alone grants you audience." He raised his hand, and the vast hall reconfigured itself around them. Walls flowed like liquid stone, columns rearranged themselves with perfect intention, until they stood in a circular chamber. Three thrones materialised – one of crystallised light, another of woven shadows, and a third of frozen starlight.

The reconfiguration wasn't mere magic but revelation—space itself responding to consciousness, showing how physical reality was merely consensual illusion, capable of fluidity when perceived differently. The chamber's circular form spoke of wholeness and completion, the thrones embodying complementary aspects of existence—illumination, mystery, and eternity—arranged to demonstrate their fundamental unity despite apparent opposition.

"Sit," The Hierophant gestured toward a simple wooden chair that appeared before Lukas. It looked startlingly ordinary among the fantastical surroundings, like a piece of reality that had wandered into a dream. As Lukas settled into it, Tonto positioned himself at his feet, an unwavering anchor to sanity.

The Emperor leaned forward, his crown of starlight casting ethereal designs across the chamber. "You have encountered Peter's influence," he stated. "Tell us of your journey. Speak of the temptations you have faced... and those to which you may have yielded."

As Lukas recounted his experiences, unseen light sources danced across the chamber, casting shadows that acted out the scenes he described. He spoke of Arcanum's distorted streets, of familiar faces transformed, of encounters with The Fool, the deceptively helpful stranger who had revealed himself as the Devil, whom Cassandra called Peter, and finally The Magician.

The Arcana exchanged loaded glances, their expressions shifting between concern, understanding, and something darker – a foreboding that made Lukas's skin crawl. The air grew thick with unspoken implications and primordial knowledge.

"Peter wears many faces in this realm," Justice explained, her sword pulsing with each word. "He is a master of deception, of illusion. Yet you have shown remarkable resilience."

"Not remarkable enough," Lukas admitted, remembering his near-surrender in the basement club, the seductive whispers promising power and oblivion.

The Hierophant raised her hand, conjuring symbols of molten gold that danced in the air like fireflies. "Strength is not measured in victories alone," she said, her voice carrying a hypnotic quality. "It is forged in struggle, tempered by failure, defined by the wisdom gained from both."

Each golden symbol embodied not arbitrary magic but emotional truths—courage appearing as a lion, wisdom as an owl, compassion as a flowing spring. They arranged themselves to show how these qualities interrelated, how one supported another, creating a visual philosophy of human growth through adversity, the transformative power of challenge itself.

A distant bell tolled, its sound rippling through the chamber like waves across a dark lake. The vibrations penetrated to Lukas's bones, carrying warning and urgency. The Emperor straightened on his throne, his gaze sweeping the chamber before settling on Lukas with crushing intensity.

"You shall have sanctuary here," he declared. "We will provide shelter, guidance, and knowledge. But know this – Peter's influence grows stronger with each passing moment. Soon you will face choices that will echo across both worlds, decisions that will shape not only your fate but the very fabric of Arcanum itself."

Tonto nudged against Lukas's foot, offering silent comfort as Justice approached, her movements creating ripples in the air that distorted the light around her. "You must understand what you face," she said, her voice carrying the weight of cosmic law. "Peter seeks to merge Arcanum and your London, not as equal realms but with Arcanum dominant. He would remake both worlds according to his vision."

"But why?" Lukas asked. "What does he gain?"

The Hierophant stepped forward, her robes shimmering with symbols that responded to his question. "Control," she said simply. "In your world, perception is constrained, limited by collective agreement and habitual blindness. In Arcanum, perception flows freely but is balanced by timeless understandings that even he must follow. By merging the realms with Arcanum ascendant, he gains the power to shape shared reality without the constraints of consensus."

"And my friends? The ones who have been... transformed?" he shot a sideways glance at Sarah. The question had been haunting Lukas since he first encountered Mike as The Fool.

The Emperor's expression softened slightly. "They are not lost, merely... overlaid. The archetypes found resonance in their souls - aspects of themselves they either embraced or suppressed. The Fool found your friend's repressed spontaneity. The Magician found your lover's carefully controlled ambition."

"We are both ourselves and more than ourselves," Justice added. "With each day in Arcanum, the balance shifts further toward the archetype and away from the person you knew. But their essence remains... for now."

The Hierophant gestured, and the air before Lukas rippled, showing him images of his friends - first as he had known them, then as he had seen them in Arcanum, then as something else entirely, something both terrifying and beautiful, beings of pure archetypal energy with only the faintest echo of humanity remaining.

These images demonstrated not transformation but revelation—showing how archetypes already existed within his friends, dormant aspects of their true nature merely coming to prominence. The process wasn't one of replacement but of emphasis, certain facets of personality magnified while others receded, the eternal principles they embodied becoming more visible as their specific human details became less dominant.

"Time moves differently here," she explained. "What feels like days to you may be weeks or merely moments in your world. But for those caught between realms, transformation is inevitable unless balance is restored."

Lukas felt a chill run through him. "How? How do I restore balance? How do I save them?"

"That," said The Emperor gravely, "is what we must teach you."

He gestured, and the chamber's dimensions shifted subtly, the walls taking on the appearance of living stained glass. Within each panel, scenes from London's history played out in reverse – the Blitz rewinding into peace, the Great Fire rebuilding itself into pristine streets, centuries of construction and demolition cycling in endless loops.

"You must understand the true nature of Arcanum's power," Justice said, stepping forward. Her sword now blazed with such intensity that Lukas had to avert his eyes. "It is not merely a parallel world, but a reflection of all possibilities, all choices, all moments that ever were or could be."

She drew her sword in one fluid motion, using its light to trace formations in the air. Where the blade passed, reality itself seemed to part like a curtain, exposing fleeting views of other Londons – one where the Romans never left, another where the sky was permanently twilight, yet another where buildings were grown rather than built.

The sword didn't create magic portals but rather cleared Lukas's perception, allowing him to see what had always been there—the simultaneous existence of all possibilities, ordinarily filtered out by habitual consciousness. The windows weren't openings to elsewhere but momentary clarifications of omnipresent reality, revelations of the multiverse eternally coexisting within a single moment of true seeing.

"Every choice creates ripples," The Hierophant added, her robes now shifting with arrangements that made Lukas's head spin. "Each decision splits reality into countless branches. Arcanum exists in the spaces between these choices, in the moments of possibility before probability collapses into certainty."

"Arcanum is not merely a place," The Hierophant continued, her symbols rearranging themselves into concentric circles of perfect symmetry. "It is perception itself—reality viewed through an unclouded lens. Your London and this realm are not truly separate, but rather the same composition experienced through different states of awareness."

She gestured, and the floating symbols transformed into two identical arrangements—one solid and concrete, the other fluid and ethereal—yet both clearly manifestations of the same underlying reality.

"Those who cannot see Arcanum walk through it daily, perceiving only what their minds are trained to accept," she explained. "But you, with your sensitivity to arrangement and meaning, have always stood with one foot in each perception. Arcanum does not exist elsewhere—it exists alongside, within, between. It is the hidden meaning behind appearance, the deeper truth underlying apparent forms."

The Emperor nodded, starlight dancing across his features. "Your scientists glimpse it in their equations, your artists in their inspirations, your musicians—like yourself—in the spaces between notes. Arcanum is the perspective that reveals connections rather than separations, relationships rather than objects."

The Emperor rose from his throne, his constellation-embroidered robes swirling with cosmic energy. "This is why Peter seeks you, Lukas. You entered Arcanum willingly, albeit unknowingly. Your choices here are uniquely powerful – unconstrained by the usual bonds of habitual perception."

Tonto moved restlessly at Lukas's feet, his wisdom-filled eyes fixed on the shifting scenes around them. The tortoise's shell seemed to absorb and reflect the magical light in bewildering ways, creating designs that spoke of deeper mysteries.

"But such power comes with terrible risk," Justice warned, sheathing her sword. The action sent a shock wave of cold through the chamber. "Peter offers shortcuts, easy paths to enlightenment that seem to bypass the fundamental laws of growth. But every such gift is a trap, every promise a chain."

A movement caught Lukas's attention—a subtle shifting of shadows in a corner of the chamber where the light seemed reluctant to penetrate. From this darkness emerged another figure, her presence simultaneously subtle and overwhelming. Where the others radiated certainty, she exuded mystery. Her gown flowed like liquid silver, constantly changing yet maintaining perfect symmetry that reflected the phases of consciousness. Her face was half-hidden behind a diaphanous veil that revealed only eyes of such profound depth that Lukas felt himself momentarily lost in their gaze.

"The Moon," The Emperor acknowledged with a respectful inclination of his head.

The Moon moved with graceful uncertainty, each step creating ripples in the air that distorted and refracted the chamber's light like thoughts distorting perception, emotions clouding reason.

"Even The Devil was not always thus," The Moon whispered, her silvery voice barely audible beneath the celestial harmony. "Peter was once a brilliant mathematician who glimpsed something he wasn't prepared to understand—a man who saw past the veil of ordinary perception and couldn't find his way back."

Her hands traced formations in the air, conjuring a nebulous image that shifted between a human silhouette and something else—someone familiar yet unrecognisable. The image showed a young man hunched over equations, his eyes feverish with discovery and terror.

"His fall was not a single moment but a progression," she continued, the words hanging in the air like mist. "He discovered that perception shapes reality—that consciousness and existence are intertwined. But instead of respecting this revelation, he sought to control it, to bend reality to his will rather than understanding his responsibility to it."

Justice nodded gravely. "What he offers as freedom is the very chain by which he himself is bound. He forgot that seeing past the veil doesn't grant the right to tear it down for all."

The Hierophant raised her hands, and the air between them filled with floating symbols that Lukas somehow understood despite never having seen them before. "Watch," she commanded softly.

The symbols began to dance, forming complex arrangements that told stories of previous seekers – those who had found their way to Arcanum and faced similar choices. Lukas saw their fates played out in abstract yet emotionally devastating detail: some transformed into beings of pure power but lost their humanity in the process, others gained everything they desired only to discover their desires had been corrupted, still others simply disappeared into the spaces between choices, becoming cautionary tales in Arcanum's endless history.

These symbolic narratives weren't just cautionary tales but explorations of how consciousness shapes reality—each story showing how intention manifests, how perspective creates experience. Some seekers tried to control reality through force, others through manipulation; some sought escape from responsibility, others craved dominance. Each story revealed not just consequences but insights into the reciprocal relationship between perception and existence.

"These are the prices paid by those who thought themselves clever enough to outwit Peter's bargains," The Emperor said, his voice heavy with primordial grief. "Even we, the Major Arcana, are bound by laws more fundamental than magic. Peter offers freedom from these laws, but such freedom is an illusion that leads only to greater bondage."

Justice moved closer to Lukas, her presence carrying the weight of ultimate truth. "You must understand: in Arcanum, perception shapes reality. Clear perception, born of genuine awareness and compassion, brings harmony between inner and outer worlds. But vision clouded by greed or fear..." She let the thought hang unfinished as shadows crawled across the walls like living things.

"Show him," The Emperor commanded, and Justice nodded gravely.

She drew her sword once more, but this time used it to cut a doorway in the air itself. Through it, Lukas saw a familiar scene: the moment he'd found the card deck in Cassandra's shop. But now he could see the invisible connections of awareness radiating outward from that single moment – golden threads of recognition stretching into infinity.

"Every shift in perception here creates ripples," The Hierophant explained, her robes now swimming with images of consciousness affecting reality. "When understanding shifts too quickly in one place, elsewhere in Arcanum, that creates imbalance. Perhaps others find their perspectives forcibly altered, or a boundary between awareness states becomes dangerously thin. The balance must always be maintained."

The Emperor waved his hand, and the vision changed to show someone experiencing a sudden transformation of consciousness. But now Lukas could see the cost – in a distant corner of Arcanum, others suddenly found their perceptions forcibly altered, their sense of self momentarily shattered as they experienced being something other than themselves.

"This is what Peter refuses to show his followers," Justice said, her voice tight with controlled anger. "He offers transcendence without growth, but genuine evolution of consciousness cannot be forced— if someone leaps ahead unnaturally, others are pulled backward to maintain balance."

Tonto butted against his foot more firmly, as if sensing his growing distress. The tortoise's presence remained steady, unchanging, a reminder that not everything in Arcanum was fluid and uncertain. When Lukas glanced down, he noticed Tonto's eyes reflected the visions but remained calm, suggesting the venerable creature had witnessed such revelations countless times before.

"But you are different," The Emperor said, fixing Lukas with his stellar gaze. "You enter each choice fully aware, seeking understanding rather than power. That makes you dangerous to Peter's plans. It also makes you valuable to us."

As they spoke, Lukas felt something shift within him - not a physical sensation, but a deepening awareness, as if layers of perception were being peeled away. He glanced at his hands and noticed that in this chamber, away from the chaos outside, he could see faint lines of light running beneath his skin, pulsing with each heartbeat.

The lines weren't supernatural phenomena but visible manifestations of his own expanding awareness—his consciousness becoming visible to itself, perception perceiving perception. His body wasn't changing but revealing its true nature as both physical form and living thought, matter and meaning inseparably intertwined.

"What's happening to me?" he asked, watching the light trace formations that resembled the constellations on The Emperor's robes.

The Hierophant smiled, though the expression held sadness. "Arcanum reveals our true natures when we are ready to see them. You are beginning to perceive the connections that bind all things - the web of meaning that underlies apparent separation."

Justice nodded, her expression softening slightly. "Your innate perception served you well in your world, allowing you to see structures and possibilities others missed. Here, that sensitivity becomes something more - the ability to perceive reality directly, unfiltered by habitual blindness."

A gentle luminescence began to fill the chamber from above, bathing everyone in a light that somehow clarified rather than blinded. Lukas looked up to see another figure descending from what had previously appeared to be ceiling but now revealed itself as infinite space.

This new presence radiated pure, clarifying light. Where the other Arcana embodied specific principles, she seemed to represent the principle of revelation itself—truth made visible, hope made tangible, direction made clear.

"The Star," The Hierophant announced with reverence.

The Star regarded Lukas with eyes that contained galaxies. When she spoke, her voice carried the precise clarity of absolute truth.

"You always had the gift of insight," The Star said, her light shifting to illuminate different aspects of the chamber as she spoke. "In your world, you translated artists' essence into words others could understand. You bridged perspectives even then, helping others see what remained invisible to ordinary perception."

Her light intensified around Lukas's hands where the lines glowed beneath his skin.

"Your work in marketing was not merely communication but translation between viewpoints," she continued. "You perceived the essence behind expression and found ways to make it visible to others. Here in Arcanum, that same ability becomes both tool and compass— the power to see beyond illusion to underlying truth."

The chamber darkened suddenly, shadows gathering in the corners like living things. Through the stained glass windows, Lukas could see storm clouds gathering, their shapes forming faces twisted in silent screams.

"Time grows short," The Hierophant announced, her symbols flickering like candles in a wind. "Peter's influence spreads, and even these halls are not forever safe from his reach."

Justice sheathed her sword once more, but kept her hand on its hilt. "Remember what we have shown you, Lukas. Remember that every perception changes reality, every awareness carries responsibility. And above all..." She paused, her eyes reflecting countless judgments passed through countless ages, "remember that not all who wear familiar faces can be trusted."

Tonto nudged Lukas's ankle gently, his timeless eyes reflecting a wisdom that transcended words. The tortoise's shell seemed to absorb the surrounding energies, creating a small zone of clarity amidst the growing shadows. In this moment of anxiety, Lukas found himself drawing strength from the creature's age-old, steadfast presence.

The storm outside intensified, wind howling through unfathomable geometries. Thunder cracked like breaking bones, and lightning illuminated grotesque shadows that shouldn't have existed.

"Go now," The Emperor commanded, rising to his full height. "But know that you carry our mark of protection. When you have need of us, seek out places where order touches chaos, where structure meets dreams. We will hear you."

With Tonto leading the way, Lukas stepped back into Arcanum's storm-wracked streets. The rain that fell wasn't water but liquid shadows, each drop carrying whispers of temptation. Ahead lay streets that twisted like fevered thoughts, and somewhere in that maze, Peter waited with a thousand familiar faces and a thousand seductive lies.

Lukas looked down at Tonto, who gazed back with timeless, unchanging eyes. The tortoise blinked once, slowly and deliberately, as if to say: You already know more than you realise. Trust your perception. See what is truly there.

Together, they stepped forward into the storm, leaving the Court of Revelations behind but carrying its wisdom in their hearts.

The real journey, Lukas realised, was only beginning.

8

The Hermit's Shadow

The air grew thin and frigid as Lukas descended the worn steps into Aldwych Station. Each breath materialised as crystalline mist, hanging suspended in defiance of natural law before dissolving into extraordinary designs. The cold emanating from the tiled walls wasn't merely physical—it carried the weight of decades, of abandoned histories better left undisturbed.

As he reached the ticket hall, subtle signs revealed that this descent was unlike any ordinary Tube journey. The vintage posters adorning the walls shifted when viewed from different angles—advertisements for products long discontinued in the real world but somehow still relevant here. They reminded him of ideas that had come in dreams but vanished upon waking. The ghostly images transformed as he passed, faded faces in the advertisements watching him with knowing eyes.

The station itself was a masterwork of architectural defiance. Each step existed in subtle rebellion against reality—corridors that stretched longer than they should, platforms that curved when they ought to be straight, their edges canted at angles that challenged conventional understanding. White tiles gave way to marble gave way to materials that had no earthly names, each transition marked by a shiver of wrongness that travelled up Lukas's spine.

Through arched passageways that twisted beyond comprehension, he glimpsed the station interior transforming. Support beams curved through dimensions that shouldn't exist, their trajectories defying comprehension. The old roundel signs depicted destinations that rewrote themselves with every heartbeat—familiar stations becoming unfathomable locations becoming familiar again, each transformation accompanied by a sound like distant trains underwater.

"I think we're almost there," Lukas murmured to Tonto, though he had no idea what 'there' might be. Something compelled him downward, a growing certainty that answers awaited somewhere in this reality-bending station's depths.

The platform below stretched both outward and inward simultaneously, its proportions belonging in an optical illusion rather than any transport architect's plans. Columns spiralled up into darkness that felt less like absence of light and more like the presence of something primeval and aware, watching with patient malevolence.

Tonto pressed against Lukas's ankle with unprecedented urgency. The tortoise's usual stoic demeanour had given way to visible distress— his wisdom-filled eyes wide and unfocused, his head extended forward in a pose that spoke of primal warning. His claws clicked against the dusty platform in an urgent rhythm that seemed to carry meaning just beyond comprehension.

"Easy, old friend," Lukas murmured, reaching down to stroke the tortoise's shell. The reassurance was as much for himself as for Tonto. The weathered carapace felt unnaturally warm beneath his fingers, pulsing with a life force that seemed to push back against the station's creeping wrongness.

The air thickened as they moved further along the platform, becoming viscous and resistant. Each breath felt like drowning in honey, sweet and suffocating. The handrail beneath Lukas's palm burned with fevered warmth, its metal surface rippling like mercury under his touch. The tiled floor began to undulate with slow, oceanic movements, as if the entire structure was breathing.

"Steady on, Tonto," he whispered, his voice distorted by the station's unfathomable acoustics. The words echoed back in languages that had died before humans learned to write. "We're almost... somewhere."

A train pulled into the station—uncannily silent, its carriages gleaming with a polish no working Underground train had ever possessed. The doors slid open without a sound, revealing a carriage that couldn't exist within the train's external dimensions. The interior wooden roof curved upwards in a perfect arch rising aloft like the arches in a cathedral disappearing into darkness that felt alive and hungry. Grimy windows each depicted scenes from Lukas's life—some remembered, some yet to come, some from paths never taken like long ago grainy stroboscopic home cine movies.

Lukas stepped into the empty carriage, Tonto following cautiously behind. He sat down on one of the wooden benches, its surface unexpectedly warm beneath him. The tortoise settled at his feet, looking up at him with eyes that carried untold aeons of knowledge. Lukas smiled down at his faithful companion, taking a moment to breathe in this strange, suspended reality.

As Lukas watched, the movies in the windows rearranged themselves, fragments coalescing to show moments from his past in perfect detail— his grandmother teaching him to cook, her arthritis-gnarled fingers guiding his through the motions; his first professional success, the spotlight hot on his face as he struggled to navigate a room of influential people through a haze of panic and exhilaration; James's expression of wonder the first time Lukas showed him his childhood home in the countryside, the moment their professional relationship had shifted into something deeper.

FORTUNES TOLD

When he looked up from Tonto, Lukas found himself no longer alone. Sitting directly across from him was a figure that appeared to be composed more of shadow than substance. With a jolt of recognition that resonated through his very being, Lukas realised he was face to face with The Hermit—one of the Arcana he had heard referenced but never before encountered in this form. Unlike The Empress or The Magician who wielded their influence openly in Arcanum's courts, The Hermit was known to be the eldest and most solitary of their number, a keeper of hidden knowledge who stood apart from their intrigues.

There was something strangely familiar about the figure, though Lukas couldn't quite place where he might have seen him before. The man appeared elderly, with a dignity that transcended his apparent years, his features partially obscured by shifting shadows and light that seemed to emanate from within rather than without.

Now, sitting before Lukas in his true Arcanum form, he radiated an aura of such profound age that it set Lukas's teeth on edge. The Hermit's form seemed constantly in flux, his outline blurring and sharpening like a radio seeking a distant station.

"You have come seeking answers," The Hermit stated, his voice resonating with frequencies that belonged to the space between stars. It wasn't a question. His form seemed to shift and flow, as if reality itself couldn't quite decide how to perceive him.

Lukas hesitated, uncertain how to address this timeless entity. "I didn't know I was seeking anything until I arrived here."

The Hermit raised a hand, the gesture rippling through dimensions Lukas couldn't name. His fingers were skeletal, almost translucent, with bones that glowed like primordial starlight. "Few seekers understand their own journeys when they begin. Knowledge comes at its own pace, in its own time."

Tonto pressed firmly against Lukas's ankle, but even the tortoise's grounding presence couldn't entirely dispel the seductive power radiating from The Hermit. The ageless entity gestured at the transformed carriage, and the air shimmered with possibilities.

The windows shifted, showing images of London—both familiar and strange. Underground tunnels that appeared on no official maps, abandoned stations repurposed for purposes no modern traveller would recognise, secret passages connecting disparate parts of the city in ways that defied conventional geography.

"I sought knowledge across many worlds," The Hermit continued, his voice softening. "But knowledge carries weight, and that weight can... transform." He gestured, and the carriage around them expanded, the walls pulling back to reveal a panoramic view of the tunnel through windows that shouldn't exist. "As you are being transformed even now."

Lukas felt a wave of vertigo wash over him as he stared out at the darkness beyond. There was no city through the window, just the dark tunnel walls, illuminated by the repetitive flashing of flickering lamps as the train passed them by, briefly revealing brickwork that writhed and shifted in unfathomable structures when caught in the momentary light.

"What am I becoming?" Lukas whispered, fear and wonder mingling in his voice.

The Hermit's form flickered like a candle in wind. "That depends on the choices you make. Every moment in Arcanum rewrites your essence. Every perception alters your nature." He moved closer, leaving trails of ghostly after-images with each step. "But I can see the structure forming within you—a resonance with the spaces between worlds, with the threshold that gives reality meaning."

"I don't understand."

"You are becoming a bridge, a conductor between realms." The Hermit's voice carried tones that vibrated through Lukas's very being. "But bridges can be crossed in either direction. You must decide which way the current flows."

Through the ghostly windows, Lukas saw the strange, twisted shadows of Arcanum's landscape, and felt a question rising to his lips. "What is this place? Really?"

The Hermit's form elongated, stretching into a column of animated darkness. "Arcanum is both more and less than you imagine. It is a reflection, yes, but also a hunger. A dream that dreams itself, feeding on the thoughts and fears and desires of those who cross its threshold." He continued. "But it is not your world. It is a parasite, wearing beauty like a mask, but it wasn't always that way."

Lukas felt truth in these words, a cold certainty that settled in his marrow. The revelation struck him with particular force—as someone who had spent his career crafting public perception, he recognised the manipulation inherent in beautiful illusions. How many times had he reframed an artist's meltdown as 'creative intensity' or recast a disastrous performance as 'avant-garde experimentation'? The thought that he might now be caught in a grander version of the same deception made him feel physically ill.

"But Cassandra... she exists in both worlds. She seems to manage it."

The Hermit's face contorted in what might have been pity, the expression rippling across features that seemed to exist in multiple places simultaneously. "Cassandra is... a cautionary tale. A prisoner of her own choosing, caught between tick and tock." His voice dropped lower, resonating with tragic knowledge. "For every day she spends in your world, she ages years in Arcanum. Decades pass in the space between moments. Centuries compress into heartbeats."

Lukas tried to absorb this terrible revelation, his mind reeling with its implications. "And Peter?" he asked, the name emerging unbidden from some intuitive part of himself. "Is he trapped in the same way?"

The Hermit's form rippled, particles of shadow reorganising themselves into new configurations. "The one you know as Peter was once a seeker much like yourself," The Hermit said, his voice heavy with primordial sorrow. "He too found the boundaries between worlds thin. But where you seek understanding, he sought control." The Hermit spoke with the weight of one who had watched Peter's journey unfold across decades, their paths crossing and diverging as Peter's power in Arcanum grew to rival even that of the ancient Arcana.

The Hermit's fingers traced formations in the air that left fading trails of light. "He was brilliant once—a visionary who glimpsed the structures underlying reality itself. In your world, they called him mad when he published his theories about malleable dimensions and perceptual distortion. His colleagues ridiculed him; academic journals rejected his work; funding dried up. Even his family abandoned him as his obsession grew."

Lukas watched as the grimy windows shifted again to show images of a young man with burning eyes, scribbling complex diagrams on any surface he could find—notebooks, walls, even his own skin. The scenes progressed, showing the man becoming increasingly dishevelled, isolated, consumed by his work.

"In desperation, he put his theories into practice," The Hermit continued. "Where others saw solid reality, he perceived the thin spots, the places where perception shapes existence. He found a way through—or perhaps created one."

The Hermit fell silent for a moment, his shadows rippling with what might have been remembered pain. Then he stood, his form stretching upward like smoke rising from an extinguished candle.

"Here," he said, moving toward the carriage door. "Let me show you."

Lukas hesitated, glancing down at Tonto. The tortoise had gone unnaturally still, his timeless eyes fixed on The Hermit with an intensity that spoke volumes.

"Come," The Hermit beckoned, opening the door between carriages to reveal another compartment beyond—empty, identical to the one they occupied, yet somehow different in ways Lukas couldn't articulate.

"And close the door behind you."

With Tonto following cautiously at his heels, Lukas crossed the threshold. As he pulled the connecting door shut behind them, the mechanical click of the lock catching was followed by an almighty bright flash that appeared to rewrite reality itself.

When Lukas's vision cleared, the carriage was gone. In its place stood a quiet suburban street at dusk. Clouds were engulfing the setting sun, casting the scene in a grey half-light that grew colder by the moment. Long shadows from garden ornaments—a stone birdbath, carefully trimmed hedges shaped like animals, a sundial on a pedestal—were fading as the sky darkened. Wind rustled through the bushes, sending leaves tumbling across neatly trimmed lawns. The air felt charged, heavy with the promise of an approaching storm.

There was something oddly familiar about this place that Lukas couldn't quite identify—a street he felt he'd seen many times before but couldn't place in his memory. Before he could examine this nagging feeling, his attention was drawn to two figures standing in the front garden of a modest semi-detached house.

"September 1973," The Hermit's voice came from everywhere and nowhere. "My last day in your world."

Lukas realised with a start that one of the figures was a younger version of The Hermit—a smart young man with hair slicked neatly to the side, and large glasses with thin gold rims that screamed of classic 70's design. He wore a tube driver's uniform: a crisply pressed blue shirt and dark waistcoat with what Lukas recognised as the familiar roundel on the chest—the iconic London Underground logo. He appeared to have just returned from work, his expression tired but brightening as he spoke to the woman beside him.

The woman had a stylish bob haircut, and wore a burnt orange skirt that fell just below her knee, paired with a knitted patterned top in autumn colours. Her smile was warm as she gazed up at Harold, her hand resting comfortably on his arm.

"That was you," Lukas said, understanding dawning. "Before you became The Hermit."

The scene unfolded before him, wind picking up as the sky continued to darken. Though the setting nagged at Lukas's memory, he found himself too engrossed in the conversation to fully explore why it seemed so familiar.

"I'd been coming to Arcanum for three weeks," The Hermit explained as the scene unfolded. "Day trips only. I always returned home by nightfall. But that day..."

"You found me," the woman was saying to Harold, her voice carrying perfectly to Lukas despite the distance. "I've been waiting for you to find your way here."

Harold's face showed confusion. "But how are you here? I left you at home this morning."

She smiled, the expression perfectly crafted to convey love and secret knowledge simultaneously. "I've always been here, Harold. This is where I truly belong. And you belong here too." She gestured at the sky, which had begun to swirl with unnatural formations. "The mathematics of reality you've always dreamed of understanding—it all makes sense in this place."

"I don't understand," Harold said, echoing Lukas's own confusion.

"This world needs you," she continued, her hand tightening on his. "I need you. But you must choose. If you return to our world, you must return alone. I cannot go with you. I've crossed too far."

Lukas felt a chill that had nothing to do with the approaching storm. The parallels to his own experiences were too precise to be coincidental. This was the template, he realised—the formation Peter had perfected and deployed against countless visitors over the decades.

Harold looked devastated. "I won't leave you. I could never leave you."

"Then stay," she whispered, leaning forward to kiss him gently. "Stay with me. Forever."

As their lips met, something shifted in the woman's form—a ripple of wrongness that Harold, lost in emotion, didn't perceive. But Lukas saw it clearly: the briefest flicker, revealing another presence beneath the loving façade.

"I'll stay," Harold whispered as they separated. "Of course I'll stay with you."

The woman's smile widened, becoming something less human, more predatory. Harold didn't notice the change, still gazing at her with devotion, but the shadows around them deepened, coalescing into something watchful and hungry.

"Excellent choice," she said, her voice subtly altering mid-sentence. By the final word, it was no longer a woman's voice but something older, masculine, triumphant. The façade fell away completely then, revealing a handsome young man with burning eyes—the same man from the earlier visions, now radiating power and satisfaction.

Harold recoiled in horror and confusion. "What—who are you? Where's—"

"She was never here," Peter said, his voice smooth with practised charm. "But I needed you to stay. Your mind—so brilliant, so adaptable. You'll make an excellent addition to our little family."

The scene began to dissolve around them, the colours bleeding away into shadow. The last thing Lukas saw was Harold's expression of devastating comprehension, the moment when understanding dawned that he had been manipulated into permanent exile from his real life, his real wife.

Another flash, and they were back in the train carriage, The Hermit sitting across from Lukas, his shadowy form more subdued now, weighted with remembered pain.

"I never saw my Martha again," The Hermit said quietly. "I became…

this. Watching as Peter perfected his techniques, as he ensnared others, as he gradually darkened Arcanum to match his own corruption."

Lukas struggled to find words. "I'm so sorry."

"It was my choice," The Hermit responded, his voice distant. "A manipulated choice, yes, but mine nonetheless. Just as yours must be. Peter will try with you what he tried with me—what he has tried with dozens of others over the decades. He will find your deepest desire, your strongest attachment, and use it against you."

"How do I resist?" Lukas asked. "If he can appear as anyone?"

"Trust nothing that offers perfection," The Hermit said. "Real love has flaws. Real life has disappointments. Real joy is transient and more precious for it." His form began to fade slightly, becoming more transparent. "My time with you grows short. The others—the Arcana—they don't know I speak with you. They have their own... arrangements with Peter."

Tonto pressed urgently against Lukas's foot, as if sensing the imminent departure.

"Remember," The Hermit said, his voice fading like distant music, "every moment here weakens your connection to your world. Every step deeper into Arcanum makes the return more difficult. Choose wisely, and... soon."

The train lurched suddenly, beginning to move with a mournful wail that seemed to come from the metal itself. Lukas grabbed a handrail to steady himself, Tonto pressing firmly against his ankle.

"Look for the inconsistencies," The Hermit called as his form began to dissolve into the shadows. "The flaws in the illusion. They're always there if you know to seek them."

The train gathered speed, hurtling through the darkness with increasing urgency. The carriage lights flickered and dimmed as the walls seemed to contract around Lukas, the wood panels creaking like ancient ships at sea. Through the windows, he could see only blackness punctuated by occasional flickers of light—maintenance lamps spaced at irregular intervals that momentarily illuminated the tunnel's brick walls in harsh, clinical bursts. Those walls, Lukas realised, weren't just a boundary but a shelter—a solid barrier between this underground realm and whatever waited in Arcanum above.

After what felt like hours compressed into minutes, the train began to slow. Cold, sterile light flooded the carriage as they approached the final station. Fluorescent tubes lined the ceiling of the platform ahead, their unforgiving glare washing away shadows and mysteries alike. The train eased to a halt with a sigh of ancient brakes, doors sliding open onto a platform occupied by ordinary commuters who moved with the automated precision of daily routine.

As Lukas gathered Tonto into his arms and moved toward the exit, The Hermit's voice reached him one final time.

"Oh, and please, if you return, send my love to Martha."

The words hung in the air as Lukas stepped onto the platform. The doors slid shut behind him with unusual finality, and the train pulled away.

Something clicked in Lukas's mind—a sudden, quiet realisation. The familiarity of the flashback wasn't just a place he'd been before, or indeed many times... but the place he'd called home on Kennington Park Road, just many years before he'd even knew of its existence.

He turned, watching the last carriage disappear around the bend with a quiet sense of wonder. He looked down at Tonto, who gazed back with timeless, knowing eyes.

"Well, Tonto," he said, bewildered. "I guess we have some news for Mrs. Patterson don't we?"

And together, they started toward the escalators, leaving behind the echoes of Arcanum's Underground, but carrying with them the weight of its truths, and the promise of a conversation with a neighbour whose connection to this strange world was perhaps one of the longest of them all.

9

Wheel of Fortune

The London Eye, or Arcanum's twisted mockery of it, cast its gaze over the city as dawn broke, watching broken rays of a early sunrise shimmering against the cold glass facade of the Shard, which even here appeared to pierce through the heavens comparable to a skeletal finger pointing at an uncaring god. Its wrought-iron frame carved dark configurations against the churning clouds, a stark silhouette simultaneously familiar and utterly wrong. Lukas felt a chill run through him—the structure reminded him of a marketing mock-up he'd once created for an album release, where he'd distorted London landmarks to evoke primal fear. But this was no digital manipulation; the real thing loomed before him, visceral and threatening. Unlike the smooth, mechanical precision of the real London Eye, this version moved with a lurching, painful rhythm, each rotation grinding backward against time itself, metal screaming against metal reminiscent of the death throes of some primordial beast.

Lukas stood on Westminster Bridge, alone save for Tonto's steadfast presence at his feet. The tortoise pressed against his ankle, a silent reassurance in this world where nothing else could be trusted. Above them, the sky of Arcanum was a canvas of unfathomable colours—deep purples that absorbed light, blues that made Lukas's eyes water, and a sickly green that evoked both decay and rebirth simultaneously. The Thames below reflected this alien firmament, its waters flowing in directions that defied natural law, sometimes splitting into multiple streams that ignored gravity entirely. Occasional ripples spread outward not from falling objects but from thoughts themselves, as if the river were listening, responding to unspoken doubts.

"I don't know if I can do this any more, old friend," Lukas murmured, his voice barely audible above the river's unnatural babbling. The weight of his journey through Arcanum pressed down upon him—each betrayal, each danger, each moment of wonder and horror had taken its toll. Exhaustion crept through his bones comparable to a slow poison. "Maybe this is where our story ends... trapped between worlds, belonging to neither."

He leaned against the cold stone railing, its rough texture shifting slightly beneath his palms, never quite maintaining the same configuration. Even this simple point of contact couldn't be trusted in Arcanum. The bridge stretched before and behind him, but its length changed with each blink, sometimes extending into unfathomable distance, sometimes contracting until the banks appeared mere steps away.

Memories flashed through his mind—the fateful card reading that had started it all, the moment London began to transform around him, his friends twisting into archetypes of themselves. The Fool dancing geometric figures beyond comprehension in Covent Garden. The Magician's betrayal in his nightclub of illusions. The Devil—Peter, he'd begun to think of him, giving the entity a name made him seem more approachable, more human somehow—always waiting, always watching, wearing James's face equivalent to a poorly fitted mask. Sometimes, in unguarded moments, Lukas caught glimpses of something surprisingly vulnerable in those borrowed features—a loneliness that conveyed both ancient and profound before the mask of confident malice slipped back into place. Peter's eyes would occasionally drift toward the horizon, as if searching for something forever lost to him.

"How do we fight something that can reshape reality itself?" he asked, not expecting an answer. "How do I lead anyone when I can barely find my own way?" The question hung in the air, heavy with the desperation of a man reaching his breaking point.

Navigating Arcanum's treacherous landscape had worn him down. Each victory had come at a cost, each step forward had been met with fresh horror.

Tonto nudged his ankle again, more insistently this time. The tortoise's wisdom-filled eyes gazed upward, not at Lukas but at the swirling sky above. Following that steady gaze, Lukas watched as the clouds began to move with deliberate purpose, coalescing into shapes that defied conventional understanding.

First came a face formed of moonlight and shadow—familiar yet transformed. The barista from the café on the corner, now rendered in celestial glory as The Moon. Her features, crafted from silver-lined clouds and patches of night sky, possessed a liquid grace that transcended physics. Yet beneath this ethereal visage, Lukas glimpsed flashes of her human expression—the same concentrated furrow of her brow that appeared when she steamed milk with perfect precision. Her eyes were craters filled with boundless depth, and when she moved, ripples spread through the heavens equivalent to stones dropped in still water. In the brief moments when The Moon's light dimmed, her human consciousness appeared to surface more fully—her tired eyes reflecting the early mornings at the café, her quick hands that once crafted intricate latte art now weaving arrangements of starlight.

"Your journey has been long, and arduous," came a voice that appeared to emanate from everywhere and nowhere, carried on a breeze that smelled of midnight gardens and distant seas. "But the path ahead holds both peril and profound revelation."

The clouds shifted again, darkness giving way to radiant light as The Sun took shape against the eastern horizon. His face, forged from early dawn and blazing gold, was that of Mr. Henderson, the proprietor of Kennington Park Road's finest greasy spoon café, transformed into something primeval and powerful. For a brief moment, the same laugh lines that appeared when he'd handed Lukas his morning takeaway coffee emerged through the celestial visage—a glimpse of the human within the archetype. Henderson's characteristic humming as he crafted latte art became the resonant hum of solar flares, his welcoming smile transformed into the majestic movement of a celestial body. When the solar brilliance occasionally dimmed, Henderson's human mannerisms would assert themselves more clearly—that habit of adjusting the cloth apron that no longer existed, his tendency to rock on his heels when speaking. Rays of actual warmth cut through the pre-dawn chill, carrying with them the scent of sun-baked earth and summer meadows.

"No need for such gloom!" The Sun's voice boomed across the Thames, momentarily silencing the river's chaotic babbling. "Stand tall, Lukas. Your burdens may be heavy, but your strength is greater still."

Between The Moon and Sun, the very stars themselves began to shift, forming constellations that had never existed on Earth. They arranged themselves into the unmistakable form of Katie, the once-harried tax consultant from his building, now rendered as The Star. Her celestial body was composed of pinpricks of light that left trailing after-images across the night sky, creating the impression of multiple versions of herself existing simultaneously. Katie's human essence manifested in the way those stars arranged themselves—her nervous energy that once had her tapping her pen during meetings now appeared as vibrating photospheres of starlight around her form. When cosmic radiation momentarily subsided, Katie's quick, analytical mind showed through in the precise geometric arrangements her stars formed, her human gestures translated into astral movements.

Lukas remembered how Katie had once praised a minimalist album cover he'd designed—'Sometimes less is more,' she'd said, unknowingly echoing the exact brief he'd been given for that avant-garde music production. Now she embodied that principle perfectly, her essence distilled to essential points of light, saying more through suggestion than any explicit detail ever could.

"The Wheel turns," The Star's voice chimed akin to distant bells, each word creating ripples of light that spread outward through the heavens. "And with it, the fabric of what you perceive as reality unwinds."

Each celestial vision was both beautiful and terrifying—familiar faces transformed into cosmic forces, yet still carrying traces of the people he had known in his ordinary life. They hovered above the river, their combined radiance casting the bridge in light that conveyed penetration beyond merely the physical darkness.

Lukas stood transfixed, caught between wonder and despair. These celestial visions were beautiful beyond words, yet their very existence reminded him how far he was from the normal world he'd once known, the London of routine and logic and predictable physics that now felt equivalent to a half-forgotten dream.

For years, he'd crafted marketing copy that promised transcendence—for albums, films, experiences—straining language to evoke what couldn't be captured in words. Now, faced with actual transcendence, he realised how hollow those carefully constructed phrases had been. How could he possibly describe the Thames flowing in two directions simultaneously? What tag line could capture the sensation of standing before beings composed of starlight and memory? This experience existed in the spaces between words, in the gaps his professional vocabulary couldn't bridge.

"Why show yourselves now?" he asked, his voice stronger than he expected. "Where were you when I was lost? When I was betrayed? When everything I thought I knew turned to lies?" The accusation hung in the air, raw with the accumulated pain of his journey.

The celestial Arcana exchanged glances, a silent communication passing between their radiant forms. The Star's constellation shifted, her stellar face showing something akin to compassion.

"We have always been here, Lukas. In the configurations of light and shadow, in the spaces between moments. But understanding comes only when one is ready to see."

"Ready?" Lukas laughed, a bitter sound that echoed strangely across the water. "I've been fighting to survive since I got here! I've watched my friends transform into strangers. I've been hunted, betrayed, tempted..." His voice cracked with emotion. "What else did I need to endure to be 'ready'?"

The Moon's silver face rippled comparable to water disturbed by wind. "Look beyond what merely is, to what could be. To what must be."

As she spoke, the surface of the Thames below began to change. No longer merely reflecting the unfathomable sky, it now showed visions of its own—a network of glowing strands that connected different points in London, pulsing with light. Some bright and vibrant, others dark and throbbing with sinister energy. Each strand whispered its own story, its own potential future.

"Each thread represents a path," The Moon explained, her words leaving trails of silver frost in the air. "Some lead to shadows, others to enlightenment. But all are equally valid. All are real, in their own way."

Lukas stared down at this liquid tapestry of possibility, overwhelmed by the multitude of choices, the weight of potential consequences. Tonto pressed more firmly against his leg, a steady, grounding pressure among these ethereal visions.

"I don't understand," he whispered, his voice small against the vastness of the revelation before him. "What am I supposed to see?"

The Sun's golden face expanded across the horizon, his warmth reaching Lukas comparable to an embrace. "You have confronted the Devil's darkness. You have seen the shadows that lurk in others. But have you truly seen the light that resides within yourself?"

There was something else in The Sun's voice, a subtle undercurrent of... pity? Or perhaps a warning. As he spoke, the waters of the Thames stilled into a perfect mirror, reflecting not the unfathomable sky but Lukas himself. Yet the reflection showed him transformed— standing tall, wreathed in a gentle golden aura, radiating a quiet, inner confidence. This wasn't the Lukas who had stumbled through Arcanum, lost and afraid. This was... something more. A potential he hadn't dared acknowledge.

"This is how we perceive you," The Sun said, his voice softer now, more intimate. The light around Lukas fractured into motes that swirled akin to fireflies, each one carrying fragmented images of possible futures. "A beacon of potential. A nexus of possibilities."

"I... I don't understand," Lukas stammered, his voice barely a whisper against the renewed babbling of the Thames. "I'm just... me."

The Star's laughter cascaded down from the heavens, a sound akin to the chiming of celestial bells that sent ripples through the fabric of reality itself. New constellations blossomed in her wake, configurations of light that had never been seen by human eyes.

"Just you? My dear boy, there is no 'just' about any living soul. You carry within you the same spark that ignites the stars themselves. The same potential for creation and destruction."

Her words struck something deep within him, a truth he had been running from since his first steps into Arcanum. He had been so focused on survival, on finding his way home, that he'd never truly acknowledged the transformation taking place within himself.

"Your career," interjected The Moon, her silvery form shifting above the river, "it always sought to shape how others see the world." Her voice carried a hypnotic quality that made Lukas's skin prickle. "That gift is what makes you dangerous to Peter... and valuable to Arcanum."

The London Eye continued its backward rotation, each turn grinding against time itself. With each revolution, the city around them changed and shifted. This was Arcanum at its most fluid, reality itself becoming malleable. Buildings stretched and contracted, streets folded in on themselves, and the boundaries between what was and what could be blurred into something undistinguishable.

The Moon's voice grew more serious, her words crystallising in the air comparable to frost. "Peter offers power, but it comes at a terrible price. A corruption of the soul, a twisting of purpose. He was not always as you see him now. Once, he too understood the delicate balance of worlds, but his yearning for certainty, for absolute control, led him down darker paths." She paused. "We do not know his ultimate aim, only that it involves unravelling the threads of order, of cohesion."

She paused, her silvery gaze conveying direct focus on Lukas despite the unfathomable distance. The temperature around him dropped suddenly, and shadows danced across the bridge with new purpose.

"We offer understanding. Truth. The ability to see the universe, and your place within it, with clarity. The choice, as always, is yours."

The words resonated with Lukas in a way nothing else had since entering this twisted realm. In all his encounters—with The Fool's chaotic energy, The Magician's seductive illusions, even Peter's tempting promises—he had been reacting, surviving. Now these celestial beings were offering him something different. Not power over others, but insight into himself.

But now, through Arcanum's lens, he could see a deeper truth in his work—configurations he had sensed without fully understanding.

Lukas bent down to reassure Tonto, who nuzzled his head into his hand, a small, insistent gesture. The tortoise's weathered shell appeared to reflect both starlight and shadow, a perfect balance of opposing forces. And in that moment, something clicked into place within Lukas's mind. It wasn't about choosing between two worlds, between magic and mundane. It was about integrating both, seeing the extraordinary within the ordinary, accepting the full spectrum of existence.

"I choose... to see," Lukas said, his voice firm, gaining strength with each word. The knot in his stomach began to unwind, replaced by a growing sense of purpose. "To see both worlds as they are. The beauty and the horror. The light and the shadow. To embrace it all."

The celestial figures appeared to exchange a look of quiet satisfaction. A silent acknowledgment passed between them, causing the very air to vibrate with potential.

"Then your understanding truly begins," they said in unison, their voices blending together in a chord that resonated deep within Lukas's soul.

The Thames below erupted in a swirling vortex of images—potential futures both terrifying and breathtakingly beautiful. Lukas saw himself leading a resistance through the twisted streets of Arcanum, saw battles fought with both magic and conviction. He witnessed moments of triumph and devastating loss, of love found and sacrificed, of creation and destruction intertwined.

The Star's constellation pulsed brighter, her presence causing the visions to shimmer and dance. "Each possibility is real," she explained, her words trailing stardust as they floated down. "Each choice creates new threads in the tapestry of existence."

The stars rearranged themselves, forming ghostly images of different versions of Lukas, each walking a different path.

The Moon's silver face rippled, and her reflected light coalesced upon the water's surface into a map of London—both versions superimposed.

"Peter's influence grows stronger," she warned, her voice carrying the chill of winter nights. Dark tendrils spread across the ethereal map, corrupting and twisting everything they touched. "He seeks to merge the worlds, but in a way that would destroy both."

On the liquid map, Lukas watched as familiar landmarks darkened, their forms twisting into nightmarish versions of themselves. Westminster Abbey's spires curved resembling claws reaching for the sky; Trafalgar Square became a whirlpool of shadows where statues wept black tears.

"But where there is darkness, there must also be light," The Sun interjected, his golden radiance pushing back the encroaching shadows. "And you, Lukas, have begun to understand the true nature of power." His warm light focused on Tonto. "Your companion has known this all along."

The tortoise's wisdom-filled eyes contained centuries of knowledge, reflecting both starlight and shadow. His presence had been constant throughout Lukas's journey, a steady anchor in a world of shifting realities.Then, something new began to happen. The celestial images wavered slightly, and through their translucent forms, Lukas glimpsed other figures—the real people beneath the Arcana. For a moment, Katie's human features showed through The Star's constellation, her familiar worried frown visible as she appeared to struggle against the archetype's cosmic power. The café owner's cheerful smile broke through The Sun's radiance, his eyes widening in confusion as if suddenly aware of his imprisonment. The barista's tired eyes peered through The Moon's silver face, her expression one of bewildered recognition. They conveyed confusion, fear, loss—human souls trapped within archetypal configurations, conscious of their entrapment yet unable to break free of the cosmic roles they now embodied.

"They're still in there," Lukas breathed. "All of them—not just echoes or projections. The real people are trapped inside the Arcana."

The celestial forms flickered more pronouncedly, as if his recognition had disturbed their cohesion. The Star's voice, when she spoke again, carried a more human quality beneath its celestial resonance.

"Help...us..." The words conveyed a struggle through layers of cosmic power.

"How?" Lukas asked urgently. "How do I free you?"

But the human presence retreated, the archetypal energies reasserting themselves. The Star's form stabilised, her constellation burning bright once more.

"The balance must be restored," she said, her voice once again purely cosmic. "The cards must be returned to their proper alignment. Only then can the separation between worlds be maintained."

Dawn began to break in earnest now, the celestial visions fading with the night. The Star spoke one final time, her voice growing distant as her constellation dimmed.

"Remember what you have seen here. The universe resides within you. As it does in all things."

"Even in the smallest, most seemingly insignificant acts of kindness," The Moon added, her silver face dissolving into ordinary clouds. Her smile was enigmatic as moonlight on water as she faded from view.

"And in every moment of courage, no matter how fleeting," The Sun concluded, his golden visage melting into the ordinary sunrise. "The power to resist darkness lies not in grand gestures, but in the everyday choice to remain true to oneself."

As the celestial Arcana disappeared, their words continued to echo in Lukas's mind. The revelation settled into him, reshaping his understanding of his journey. He had been searching for a way home, for an escape from Arcanum's dangers, but perhaps that had never been the true purpose of his crossing between worlds. Perhaps he had needed to see reality through Arcanum's distorted lens to recognise the magic that had always existed in his ordinary life—the beauty of morning light on brick, the miracle of human connection, the small kindnesses that went unnoticed.

And perhaps Arcanum needed him—his perspective, his choices, his peculiar blend of pragmatism and wonder—to push back against the corruption Peter spread.

Lukas took a deep breath, feeling a new kind of strength flow through him. It wasn't the raw power that Peter had offered, but something more fundamental—clarity. Purpose. Understanding.

The ordinary dawn light caught on Tonto's shell, highlighting configurations that conveyed more than just the tortoise's life. In those age-old grooves, Lukas saw reflections of his own journey, of all journeys—moments of joy and sorrow, triumph and defeat, all woven together into something beautiful precisely because of its imperfection.

"Thank you, old friend," he said softly, kneeling to stroke Tonto's weathered shell. "For staying with me. For showing me the way."

The tortoise blinked slowly, his wisdom-filled eyes reflecting a knowledge that transcended worlds. His steady presence had been the one constant in a realm of perpetual change, a tether to truth when illusions threatened to overwhelm.

As Lukas straightened, he noticed a difference in the air around him—a subtle shift in the energy of Arcanum itself. Before, the realm had felt hostile, its twisted reality a trap designed to ensnare him. Now it felt… responsive. Not friendly, exactly, but more akin to a musical instrument awaiting a skilled hand. The city's unfathomable architecture no longer conveyed mockery but instead waited, attentive, for his next move.

From the early morning mist on the bridge, shapes began to emerge—familiar figures moving with purpose through the thinning fog. They approached cautiously at first, then with growing confidence as they recognised him.

The High Priestess emerged first, her white robes flowing akin to liquid moonlight. She had been Maya, the librarian from near his house. Now, her eyes held the unsettling wisdom of centuries, though occasionally they would blink with Maya's characteristic nervousness. When she gestured with her hands, there was Maya's precise movement—the way she'd once shelved books with careful attention—translated into arcane significance. In moments of concentration, her human consciousness conveyed closer proximity to the surface, manifesting in the slight tilt of her head that Maya always used when contemplating a difficult reference question.

"We felt the shift," she said, her voice resonating with newfound authority. "Something has changed. You have changed."

The Chariot followed, the morning light gleaming off his ethereal armour. In his ordinary life, he had been Detective Inspector Matthews. Here in Arcanum, that investigative quality had transformed into something more literal—a warrior's resolve, a champion's courage. Yet the same analytical squint with which he'd examined evidence now assessed the shifting landscape around them. Matthews's methodical approach to cases now expressed itself in the precise, tactical way The Chariot positioned himself, his human habits of tapping fingers against his thumb when thinking translated into a rhythmic adjustment of his spiritual armour.

"Peter's influence has been pushed back," he observed, his gaze scanning the horizon. "Not defeated, but... contained, for the moment."

Strength approached, her lion padding silently beside her. When she spoke, her voice carried a gentle yet firm quality.

"You've found your centre," she said, her voice gentle yet firm. "It changes everything."

One by one, they gathered—The Hermit, Justice, The Emperor, Temperance—each a transformed reflection of someone Lukas had known in his ordinary life. Each now embodying an archetypal truth, yet still carrying flashes of their former personalities. They formed a circle around him on the bridge, their combined presence creating a pocket of stability in Arcanum's shifting landscape.

"Peter's influence is strongest in the east," the High Priestess announced, her gaze turning toward the rising sun. "His corrupted Arcana have taken hold there."

The Chariot nodded, pointing toward a section of the city where the distortions were most pronounced. "The buildings are changing faster there, becoming more twisted. Reality itself is unravelling at its edges."

A distant roar echoed across the Thames, a sound conveying no resemblance to any earthly creature Lukas had ever heard. It sent vibrations through the bridge, causing ripples in the river below that moved against the current.

"His forces grow bolder," Strength observed, her hand resting on her lion's flank. "They feel threatened by what happened here." The Hermit stepped forward, his lantern casting a light that conveyed piercing through the very fabric of reality. "Peter is not merely angry," he said, his voice carrying the weight of contemplation. "He is afraid. Each person you free diminishes his control, reveals the fragility of the world he's constructed."

Lukas looked at their faces—these transformed reflections of ordinary people now battling for Arcanum's soul. Their expressions showed determination tinged with fear, courage undercut by doubt. They were looking to him not just for leadership but for hope.

And yet, beneath their archetypal aspects, he could now perceive the trapped human essences within—frightened, confused, pulled between worlds. Their human souls were conscious captives, aware on some level of their imprisonment within these powerful but alien forms. It wasn't just his closest friends who needed saving—it was everyone in Arcanum who had been transformed.

Drawing on his new understanding, Lukas spoke with quiet confidence, "We'll divide our forces. The High Priestess, take The Hermit and Justice along the Thames. The Chariot, you and Emperor circle from the north. Strength and I will take the central route with Tonto."

His words carried a weight they hadn't before, as if Arcanum itself responded to his newfound clarity. The twisted spires of Westminster conveyed straightening slightly, the unfathomable angles of the bridge stabilised beneath his feet.

"Peter's agents will anticipate caution," Strength said, her lion's eyes gleaming with tactical insight. "Sometimes the most direct path is the least expected."

They moved through London's transformed landscape with new purpose, navigating streets that folded back on themselves and buildings that breathed akin to living things. Arcanum's reality remained fluid, but now it conveyed less hostility—more akin to an ocean with dangerous currents than an actively malevolent force.

As they approached Covent Garden, the distortions intensified. Market stalls floated a foot above the cobblestones, their wares shifting between mundane produce and shimmering, otherworldly orbs. The air crackled with tension, and shadows whispered as they passed.

"There," Strength pointed toward the Royal Opera House, its once-elegant facade now twisted into a grimacing mask. "The corruption is concentrated there."

The building's columns writhed akin to serpents, and its windows reflected geometric configurations that defied natural explanation. A darkness emanated from within—not the absence of light, but something more conscious, more deliberate. Shadows pooled at its entrance, occasionally forming shapes that suggested faces, limbs, claws.

"They've sensed us," Lukas said quietly, feeling the weight of invisible eyes upon them. Tonto pressed against his ankle, his weathered shell vibrating with a subtle warning.

The darkness at the Opera House entrance congealed, taking form. Figures stepped out—people Lukas recognised, though their features had been twisted by Peter's influence. Tom, the cheerful barista who always remembered Lukas's order, now moved with jerky, puppet-like motions, his smile stretched too wide, his eyes gleaming with malice. The darkness of Peter's corruption clung to him comparable to a second skin, seeping from his pores and trailing behind him resembling smoke. What had once been Tom's graceful barista movements—the elegant pour of coffee, the artistic swirl of cream—were now contorted into unnatural gestures that mimicked his former self but lacked all genuine warmth.

Behind him came others—the florist from the corner, the teacher from the community centre, the elderly man who walked his dog in the park every morning—all transformed into corrupted versions of themselves, darkness seeping from their pores resembling smoke. Each one moved with that same unnatural rhythm, their personalities suppressed beneath Peter's influence, yet occasionally their true selves would surface—a familiar gesture, a characteristic expression quickly consumed by the corruption that possessed them.

"Look what wandered into our web," Tom said, his voice grating comparable to broken glass, though undertones of his human voice occasionally broke through resembling someone drowning calling for help. "Peter told us you might come this way." His hands, once skilled at creating intricate latte art, now dripped with a substance that resembled oil but moved with deliberate purpose. "He wants to speak with you, Lukas. He has an offer you really shouldn't refuse."

The corrupted Arcana spread out, forming a semicircle that blocked their path. Each moved with unnatural grace, as if their bodies were merely vessels for something else, something that didn't quite understand how human limbs should work.

"Your master has nothing I want," Lukas replied, his voice steady despite the dread pooling in his stomach. "And you don't belong to him either, Tom. None of you do."

Tom's face twisted in rage, the expression too extreme for his features. But beneath that rage, Lukas caught a flicker of something else—fear, confusion, a desperate cry for help. For a moment, Tom's true eyes peered through the mask of corruption, silently pleading. The darkness receded momentarily from his face, showing the trapped consciousness within that remained aware of his imprisonment, helplessly watching as his body acted against his will.

"Such arrogance!" Tom spat, though the words conveyed recitation, as if forced. "Peter offers power without limits, freedom from the mundane world's constraints. Why do you resist? What does your… humanity… offer that compares?"

The question hung in the air, a challenge that demanded an answer. Lukas thought of the celestial Arcana's revelations, of the potential futures he'd glimpsed in the Thames, of Tonto's unwavering presence beside him. He thought of his ordinary life back in London—morning coffee on his steps, music filling his house, the simple joy of watching the city wake up.

"It offers connection," he said finally, the words coming from a place of certainty he hadn't known he possessed. "Real connection, not just power over others. It offers compassion. Growth. The chance to be something more than what you were yesterday."

He took a step forward, and to his surprise, the corrupted Arcana shifted back slightly, as if his words carried physical force. He recognised this moment—it was akin to when he'd convinced a sceptical record executive to back an unknown band by helping him see beyond preconceptions, by reshaping perception itself.

"Look at yourselves," he continued, seeing uncertainty flicker across their distorted faces. "Is this what you wanted? To be puppets? To have your essence corrupted for someone else's agenda?"

Tom's sneer faltered, a flicker of his true self showing through Peter's influence. The darkness around him swirled in agitation, as if fighting to maintain its hold. The corruption that had seeped into him through promises of power and significance—whispered enticements that had played on his desire for recognition beyond his barista counter—now visibly weakened as his authentic self fought for control.

"There is always a price," Lukas pressed, drawing strength from Tonto's presence beside him. Every lesson he had learned, every betrayal he had endured, every moment of fear and wonder, coalesced into this single, defiant moment. "Peter didn't tell you that, did he? Everything he offers comes with chains attached. But you can choose differently. You can remember who you really are."

Strength stepped forward, her lion letting out a roar that shook the very foundations of the distorted reality around them. The sound was pure, untainted truth, a primal force that resonated with a power Peter's corruptions couldn't match.

Three of the corrupted Arcana cried out, falling to their knees as the darkness receded from their forms comparable to a tide pulled back by an unseen moon. Their faces cleared, awareness returning to their eyes as they remembered who they had been before the corruption.

The teacher gasped, looking at her trembling hands as the oily darkness that had seeped through her skin dissipated akin to morning mist. The elderly dog walker blinked rapidly, tears streaming down his weathered cheeks as his consciousness fully returned to him, the memory of his willing submission to Peter's temptation bringing shame and relief in equal measure.

"The Devil's hold can be broken!" Lukas called out, his voice filled with desperate hope. "You don't have to be what the cards have made you! You can choose!"

Tonto moved amongst them, his slow, deliberate progress a counterpoint to the chaotic energy of the confrontation. Each touch of his shell, each seemingly insignificant nudge, conveyed anchoring them, pulling them back from the precipice of oblivion. The tortoise's wise gaze identified those most receptive to freedom, those whose inner light still flickered beneath the corruption.

The corrupted florist—Emma—looked down at her hands. The darkness that had dripped from them was receding, revealing her normal skin beneath. The corruption that had taken root when she'd accepted Peter's offer—his promise that she could create flowers that would never die, that would bring unfathomable beauty to the world—now faded as she remembered the simple joy of nurturing living things, of accepting their natural cycle of growth and decay.

"What... what happened to me?" she whispered, horror and wonder mixing in her voice. "I remember agreeing to something... he said I could create perfect beauty that would last forever..."

"You were used," Strength explained gently, helping the woman to her feet. "But that doesn't define you. Your choices from this moment forward—those define you."

Tom's scream of frustration cut through the air, the sound inhuman in its rage. The darkness around him intensified, forming into tendrils that lashed out resembling whips. His corruption ran deeper than the others', Peter having exploited his deep-seated desire for recognition, his bitterness at being overlooked despite his talents.

"This... this is not over!" he snarled, his voice cracking with desperation as his control over the others waned. "Peter sees everything! He knows your deepest fears, your secret shames! He will use them against you!"

For a moment—just a flicker—Tom's expression changed. Something vulnerable, almost childlike, surfaced in his eyes. "He understands what it's like to be trapped between worlds," Tom whispered, his voice suddenly his own again. "He's been searching for so long..."

Then the darkness surged back, consuming him from within. With that, he dissolved into a swirling mass of shadows that slithered away between the distorted cobblestones, disappearing into the labyrinthine depths of Arcanum.

The remaining corrupted Arcana, those who hadn't been freed, followed in his wake, leaving behind an echo of their tormented screams.

The liberated ones huddled together, shaken by their ordeal. The teacher stared at her trembling hands. "I remember... serving him. Willingly. I thought he was offering enlightenment, but it was just another kind of prison."

Lukas nodded, understanding all too well Peter's manipulative methods. "He twists your deepest desires into traps. Makes freedom look like a cage and captivity feel like liberation."

"There will be others," the elderly dog walker said, his eyes clearer now but haunted by what he'd experienced. "Many others who accepted his offer, who still believe his lies."

"And we'll help them too," Lukas promised, looking around at the small victory they'd achieved. "One by one if necessary."

From other parts of the city, reports began to filter in—carried by birds with too-intelligent eyes, by shadows that moved against the light, by the wind itself which conveyed whispering messages directly into their minds. The other teams had engaged Peter's forces and achieved similar, limited successes.

The corrupted Opera House had begun to straighten, its columns no longer writhing in pain, though darkness still leaked from its windows resembling smoke. The very fabric of Arcanum itself was responding to these small victories. Streets that had once twisted into painful geometric impossibilities now occasionally resolved into recognisable thoroughfares. The sky, though still alien in its colouration, showed patches of familiar blue between the swirling arrangements.

Each freed soul conveyed anchoring reality, pulling it back toward normality one fragment at a time.

"We have won this battle," Lukas acknowledged, his voice weary but tinged with newfound determination. "But the war... the war for the soul of Arcanum, and perhaps for something far greater... is far from over. Peter will return. He will wear new faces, offer new temptations."

Justice stepped forward, her scales gleaming in the half-light. "His world is built on deception. Even the smallest truth weakens his foundations."

Tonto nudged Lukas's ankle, a gentle, persistent pressure. Lukas looked down at his faithful companion and smiled, a genuine smile that reached his eyes. "Yes, old friend," he said softly. "We'll be ready. We have to be."

Above them, Big Ben, its hands still moving backward, chimed an unfathomable hour. The sound echoed through the distorted streets, marking time in a realm where reality itself was a constantly shifting, negotiable construct.

As if to confirm this unspoken thought, a single, elongated shadow, detached from any visible source, stretched across the cobblestones, lingering for a moment too long before fading away—a chilling reminder that the fight was far from over.

The freed Arcana gathered around them, their forms solidifying as they remembered who they truly were. In their eyes, Lukas saw both gratitude and determination. They had tasted Peter's power and rejected it, choosing instead the harder path of remaining true to themselves. It was a small victory, perhaps, but a significant one.

Lukas lifted Tonto onto the nearby wall to see more clearly the gathering crowd. He stood resting his hand on Tonto's shell, feeling its reassuring warmth. The celestial Arcana's revelations echoed in his mind—that true power came not from changing reality, but from seeing it clearly; that the universe resided within him as it did in all things; that even the smallest acts of kindness and courage could push back against darkness.

He looked out at the city—still distorted, still dangerous, but now somehow more approachable. Not an enemy to be defeated, but a realm to be healed, one choice at a time. And with each such choice, each person freed, each truth remembered, another thread was woven into the fabric of resistance against the darkness that threatened both worlds.

In the distance, beyond the twisted spires of Arcanum's skyline, the silhouette of the Tower loomed—tall, imposing, and conveying impervious to the changes rippling through the rest of the city. Something awaited him there, Lukas knew. A confrontation that would define not just his fate, but the fate of both worlds.

But for now, this small victory was enough—these freed souls, this reclaimed piece of Arcanum, this growing resistance against the darkness.

10

The Tower Falls

The Tower of London, time-weathered guardian of history, convulsed with malevolent energy. Its stones pulsated with an otherworldly glow - not the warm flicker of torchlight, but a sickly, living luminescence that spread resembling veins through the mortar. Lukas felt a sickening recognition—the Tower was transforming into something akin to the nightmarish draft concept he'd once created for a promotional campaign, where he'd envisioned London's landmarks as living, sentient entities. An idea so disturbing that his clients had rejected it immediately, preferring his more conventional designs. Now that rejected vision towered before him, viscerally real. Each pulse sent ripples through reality itself, making the air shimmer and distort as if viewed through heat waves, leaving him nauseated and disoriented. The very atmosphere vibrated with wrongness, a dissonance that penetrated bone and tissue, that made him want to cover his ears though the assault came from within as much as without.

The storm surrounding it was no mere weather – it was a symphony of chaos, a deliberately orchestrated assault on sanity. Lightning didn't just illuminate; it tore wounds in the fabric of the sky, leaving after-images that burned like acid in Lukas's vision. Each flash revealed geometric formations in the clouds above that defied natural explanation - spiral configurations that twisted in on themselves, vast shapes that conveyed watching the proceedings below with malevolent intelligence.

The thunder came not as rolls or crashes but as metallic screams, as if the very foundations of reality were being torn apart. Each blast shook loose more of the Tower's time-weathered stones, sending them floating upward instead of falling, defying gravity in ways that made Lukas's mind rebel against what his eyes were seeing. The stones didn't simply float - they rotated slowly, revealing centuries of hidden inscriptions that glowed with their own inner light, each one telling a different story of betrayal and darkness.

Lukas stood at the forefront of a small army of freed Arcana. Since the confrontation at the Opera house had been filled with a desperate campaign to liberate more of those trapped by Peter's influence. Each victory had strengthened their forces, each person freed becoming a weapon against the corruption.

"This is where we stand," he told his assembled allies, his voice steady despite the chaos surrounding them. "The Tower represents Peter's strongest hold over Arcanum. If we can break his power here, we can begin truly healing this realm."

The plan had been carefully constructed - groups of freed Arcana would attack from multiple sides, while Lukas, accompanied by those closest to the Major Arcana, would approach from the water. Tonto, as always, would guide them through the Tower's ever-changing interior to find Peter's sanctum.

"Remember," Lukas continued, "we're not fighting to destroy, but to restore balance. Our goal isn't just to defeat Peter, but to heal the rift between worlds."

Justice - the transformed Sarah - stepped forward, her form surrounded by a balanced aura of fairness and equilibrium. "What is unbalanced must be restored," she said, her voice resonating with judicial certainty. "What was taken must be returned. What was corrupted must be cleansed."

Beside her, The Chariot nodded grimly, his armour shifting resembling liquid metal in the strange light. "My forces are ready. We will create the diversion you need."

As they spoke, the Thames behind them began to churn, its waters forming into liquid stairs that would allow them to approach the Tower from an unexpected angle. The Hierophant, who had been guiding newly freed Arcana, raised her staff in blessing. "May the true configurations guide your steps," she intoned.

At Lukas's side, Sarah nodded grimly, her features occasionally flickering between her human self and her Justice aspect. "Are you sure this will work?" she asked quietly, so only he could hear.

"No," Lukas admitted. "But it's the best chance we have." He knelt beside Tonto, the faithful tortoise who had been his guide through all of Arcanum's dangers. "Ready, old friend?"

Tonto's wise gaze met his with steady certainty. There was no fear there, only determined purpose. The tortoise had been growing stronger as Arcanum's corruption receded, his shell now glowing with a subtle inner light that pushed back against the darkness.

"Then let's begin," Lukas said, rising to his feet. He drew The Tower card from his pocket, feeling its power pulse against his palm. With a deep breath, he faced the corrupted fortress and stepped onto the first liquid stair.

At the heart of this nightmare, Lukas stood with his carefully assembled allies arrayed around him. Sarah, embodying Justice, stood with arms outstretched, one hand holding scales that rippled with an oily, iridescent sheen that made his stomach turn. The corruption spread visibly along her sword resembling living tar, each droplet fell hissing and smoking where it struck the ground. Beside him, Tonto shifted restlessly, his venerable claws scraping against stones that conveyed whispering with each touch. The tortoise's unease was palpable, manifesting in ways Lukas had never witnessed before. His usually steady movements had become erratic, his head swaying from side to side as if trying to track multiple threats at once. The shell, which had always been a source of calm stability, vibrated with a frequency that set Lukas's teeth on edge.

More concerning than Tonto's physical agitation was the look in his knowing eyes. Those eyes, which had guided Lukas through countless perils in Arcanum, now held a profound dread that chilled him to his core. The tortoise's gaze darted between their supposed allies, tracking each subtle movement with the wariness of prey watching predators.

"We are prepared," whispered The High Priestess, her ethereal glow pulsing erratically. Once a source of hope and guidance, her light now fluctuated between blinding brilliance and consuming darkness, each transition accompanied by a high-pitched whine at the edge of hearing. The very air around her conveyed crystallising and shattering with each pulse, sending fragments of frozen light tinkling to the ground.

Above them, The Hierophant raised her staff, sending a beam of fractured light into the storm clouds. The light splintered and twisted, looking more akin to shards of broken reality than illumination. Where the beams touched the age-old stones, they left behind traces of equations and symbols that squirmed and reformed themselves into new arrangements, each more disturbing than the last.

They began their ascent deeper into the Tower's corrupted heart. The corridors writhed and twisted, defying conventional geometry. What should have been straight passages bent at unfathomable angles, creating spaces that couldn't exist in normal reality. Lukas found himself walking on walls, then ceilings, his sense of orientation completely destroyed. The very concept of up and down became meaningless in this violated space.

Tapestries along the walls flickered with scenes of horror – histories rewriting themselves before Lukas's eyes. He saw Anne Boleyn rising from her execution, head in hands, dancing a macabre waltz with her executioner. Ravens with human eyes pecked at the bones of forgotten prisoners, their caws forming words in dead languages. Each scene was more disturbing than the last, showing not just what had been, but what could have been, what should never be.

Tonto stopped suddenly, his claws gouging deep into stone that had become soft as clay. The sound he made was unlike anything Lukas had heard from him before – a deep, guttural warning that spoke of primal fear. The tortoise's knowing eyes, usually wells of wisdom and patience, were wide with terror. His head drew back into his shell slightly, but he stood his ground, positioning himself between Lukas and the others in a protective stance that spoke volumes.

"There is no time for hesitation," Sarah declared, her voice stripped of all humanity. When she turned to face them, her features conveyed slipping and shifting, comparable to wax melting in extreme heat. Around her, the scales of justice dripped darkness that ate through the floor, revealing glimpses of boundless depths below. "Our destiny awaits."

They reached the chamber at the Tower's apex, where reality truly began to break down. Windows showed unfathomable views – one displayed a sun-drenched morning, another the depths of midnight, while a third conveyed looking out onto a London that had never existed, where St. Paul's Cathedral rose resembling a mountain of bleeding obsidian. Each view shifted and changed when not directly observed, resembling quantum states collapsing and reforming with each blink.

In the centre of the chamber, a ritual circle pulsed with sickly green light. The symbols within it were twisted things that hurt to look at, corrupted figures that whispered madness into the mind of anyone who studied them too long. The crystals they'd gathered, once pure vessels of power, now throbbed with an internal rot that conveyed spreading through the very air.

The betrayal unfolded with terrible grace. Directly in front of Lukas, Sarah's sword glowed with a sickly light, but for a moment, Lukas caught a glimpse of darkness rippling along its edge - so brief he might have imagined it. Her smile remained warm, but something flickered behind her eyes, quick as mercury.

To his right, Mike's chaotic unpredictability twisted into nightmarish abominations, while across the chamber, The Hierophant's holy robes dissolved to reveal a skeletal form beneath, face frozen in a silent scream. The air filled with the sound of breaking glass as reality itself conveyed shattering around them, revealing the truth that had been hiding behind these familiar faces all along.

"Did you truly believe, dear Lukas," Peter spoke through them all at once, the voices surrounding Lukas from all sides as they harmonised into a chord of malevolence tinged with something else—perhaps desperation? "That I would allow you to disrupt my carefully constructed reality?" Each word resonated with multiple layers of sound, from the highest crystalline notes to subsonic rumbles that made internal organs vibrate in sympathy. For a moment, the calculated menace faltered, and Peter's true voice emerged, conveying from directly above Lukas, singular and almost pleading: "This realm took centuries to perfect—do you know what it's like to craft a world where nothing is bound by tedious constraints? Where pure imagination reigns?" The momentary vulnerability vanished as quickly as it had appeared, subsumed again by the chorus of controlled malice.

The floor cracked and buckled, revealing swirling voids of colours beyond natural explanation. Colours that had no names in any human language, colours that suggested concepts rather than light wavelengths

– the darkness of betrayal, the shade of lost hope, the hue of breaking trust. The Tower's stones groaned in protest as chunks of masonry began to float upward, forming a slowly rotating maze around them. Each piece cast shadows that moved independently, reaching with grasping fingers toward Lukas.

"Your trust was your weakness," Peter continued, each of Lukas's former allies moving with puppet-like jerks. Their faces flickered between their familiar forms and something darker, older – masks of primeval evil wearing the skin of friendship. "I merely reflected your desires back at you, letting you see what you wanted to see. And now…"

The chamber shuddered violently. The ceiling peeled away resembling the lid of a tin can, revealing a sky that wasn't a sky at all but a writhing mass of impossibilities. Reality began to tear, revealing glimpses of Arcanum's true nature – a realm of shifting geometries and unnatural architectures. Through a rent in space, Lukas saw the Thames flowing upward resembling a reverse waterfall, its waters black as ink and filled with writhing, silvery fish that spelled out prophecies with their movements.

Each tear in reality showed a different horror: Victorian London burning under a blood-red sun, the streets of Westminster populated by shadows wearing human faces, Tower Bridge twisted into an endless loop of eternal torment. But worse than the sights were the sounds – the screams of a city being unmade, the laughter of things that had never been human, the wet slithering of realities sliding against each other resembling tectonic plates of nightmare.

Tonto butted Lukas's foot with fierce determination, offering solidarity in the chaos. The tortoise's presence was the only real thing left, the only anchor in a world coming undone. Their eyes met, and in that moment, Lukas saw not just understanding but a fierce determination in those knowing orbs. Tonto's shell began to glow with a warm, steady light – not the corrupted illumination of Arcanum, but something older, purer, a defiance against the entropy surrounding them.

"Join us," Peter offered through Sarah's lips, her smile now too wide, filled with teeth that conveyed multiplying as Lukas watched. Each tooth reflected a different memory of their friendship. "You're a creator, Lukas, as I once was. You understand the frustration of having visions no one else can see, of trying to express what language and convention can't contain." Sarah's face softened momentarily, and Lukas caught a glimpse of someone else looking through her eyes—not the Devil of biblical fear, but a man who had once stood where Lukas stood now, making a different choice. "Embrace the power of Arcanum. Become one with the chaos that you've been fighting so desperately. Here, your creations can live and breathe beyond the flat limitations of page and screen."

The offer hung in the air resembling poison, seductive and deadly. Through Mike, Peter whispered promises of carefree adventure and untethered imagination, each word accompanied by visions of potential futures where Lukas ruled over vast domains of twisted reality. Through The Hierophant, it spoke of destiny and inevitability, each syllable carrying the weight of centuries of accumulated corruption.

The Tower continued its unfathomable collapse around them, stones floating upward to form a kaleidoscopic dome of rotating masonry. Each stone contained reflections of Lukas's journey through Arcanum - distorted mirrors of every choice, every mistake, every moment of doubt. One stone reflected a fortune teller in Portobello market, her weathered hands laying down the Tower card, warning of destruction that preceded transformation. Something familiar stirred in Lukas's subconscious, 'Sometimes,' her voice echoed in his distant memory, 'what seems like collapse is actually liberation.' The stone's reflection shifted to show the Tower card itself, with figures falling from a lightning-struck structure—exactly as he was experiencing now, prophecy manifesting as reality.

But as reality fractured around them, something crystallised within Lukas. He looked down at Tonto, his faithful companion through all this madness, and understood at last.

"No," he said, standing firmly in the centre of the chamber with Tonto at his side, his voice quiet but gaining strength with each word. "I choose truth over illusion. Reality over corruption. I choose to restore what you've broken."

"You understand nothing!" Peter roared through his puppets, their voices cracking with a fury that barely masked something more personal—something that might have been hurt. "This realm is mine! These souls are mine!" For a heartbeat, his unified front fractured, and Lukas glimpsed not a devil but a creator defending his life's work. "I was like you once," Peter's voice dropped to a whisper that somehow cut through the chaos more effectively than his shouts. "A mathematician who saw configurations where others saw randomness, an artist trapped between worlds. I found freedom here." The moment of revelation passed, his rage reasserting itself. "You are nothing but a lost child playing with forces beyond your comprehension!"

Lukas reached for the Tarot deck in his pocket, feeling its familiar weight. The cards were warm to the touch, pulsing with their own rhythm that conveyed countering the chaotic energy around them. Yes, they were imbued with Arcanum's power, with Peter's influence – but they were also tools, and tools could be turned against their maker.

The chamber's destruction accelerated. Windows on all sides shattered inward, their glass transforming into butterflies with razor wings that swirled in deadly configurations. The ceiling directly overhead dissolved into a swirling vortex of colours that hurt to look at, while the floor beneath their feet became a shifting mosaic of scenes from Lukas's own memories, each one twisted and corrupted.

Tonto moved with surprising speed, his claws leaving trails of golden

THE TOWER FALLS

light in the stone as he circled Lukas protectively, positioning himself between Lukas and the approaching puppets. Each step conveyed creating a small zone of stability, a bubble of reality where Peter's influence couldn't quite reach. The tortoise's primeval magic, subtle but unshakeable, began to push back against the chaos.

"I won't be your puppet," Lukas declared, drawing the first card from his deck. It blazed with light, true light, cutting through Peter's illusions. "I've seen what real power is – it's not in your tricks and transformations. It's in choice. In friendship. In love."

Each word struck Peter resembling a physical blow, causing ripples of disruption through its manifestations. The puppeteer'ed forms of his friends shuddered, momentarily showing glimpses of their true selves beneath the corruption. Sarah's eyes cleared for just a moment, showing recognition and regret. Mike's fingers twitched against his will, forming a familiar gesture of friendship.

Peter snarled, his voice now dropping all pretence of humanity. Through all its puppet-forms at once, it spoke in a language that made reality itself scream in protest. The walls of the Tower began to fold in on themselves, creating unfathomable angles and deadly geometries. Each fold revealed new horrors - glimpses of other worlds where Peter had already won, where London had become a playground of nightmares.

But Lukas held his ground, kneeling, one hand on Tonto's shell, the other gripping his cards. With each card he drew, a different kind of power manifested - not the corrupt energy of Arcanum, but something purer, drawn from his own experiences and choices. The Star card blazed with true starlight, burning away shadows. The Moon card released silver streams that wrapped around Peter's constructs, revealing their true nature.

As Lukas drew the Sun card, he felt a surge of creative energy unlike anything he'd experienced before. It wasn't the manic, boundary-breaking inspiration Peter had tempted him with, but something deeper and truer - the kind of creativity that comes from understanding one's own limitations and working within them to express something authentic. The card blazed with golden light that formed into musical notation around him - a complex structure revealing arrangements that mirrored the very mathematics of reality itself.

The notation swirled around him, gaining substance, each note striking the corrupted Arcana resembling physical blows. Where they connected, corruption receded, revealing glimpses of his real friends beneath the archetypal masks. For a moment, Mike's true face showed through the Fool's wild expression, his eyes wide with recognition.

"Lukas?" he gasped, fighting against the possession. "What's happening?"

"Hold on!" Lukas called to him, the music growing stronger around them. "Fight it! Remember who you are!"

Tonto's presence grew stronger, his venerable power harmonising with Lukas's newfound strength. The tortoise's shell began to emit a deep, resonant hum that counteracted Peter's discordant symphony. Where their combined power touched, reality began to heal, to straighten, to remember its proper shape.

Peter's puppets attacked in unison, their movements a blur of unfathomable angles and corrupted power. From the centre of the chamber, Sarah's scales tilted wildly, sending waves of corrupted judgment through the air.

But for each attack, Lukas had a defence - not just in the cards he wielded, but in the memories and truths they represented. Standing his ground at the centre, he met Sarah's chaos with The Justice card, its light revealing the true nature of balance and forcing her to confront her own place within the order of things. Pivoting to face his right, against Mike's wild, unpredictable magic, he raised The Hermit, its quiet wisdom dispersing illusions. Spinning around to face the threat behind, The Hierophant's dark power shattered against The High Priestess, whose mysteries were deeper and truer than any corruption.

The battle transformed the chamber into a maelstrom of competing realities. Chunks of the Tower spun through the air resembling planets in a miniature solar system, each one showing a different version of events. Lightning from the storm outside struck inward instead of outward, creating a cage of electric fire around them all.

"You understand nothing!" Peter roared through its puppets, their voices cracking with fury. "This realm is mine! These souls are mine! You are nothing but a lost child playing with forces beyond your comprehension!"

"No," Lukas replied, his voice steady despite the chaos. "I understand everything now. You don't own this realm - you're just another prisoner of it, trapped by your own need to control, to corrupt, to destroy. But there's something you can never corrupt."

With the battle raging around them, he knelt beside Tonto, placing one hand on the tortoise's shell while holding his cards with the other. The contact sent waves of warmth through him, reminding him of every moment they'd shared, every quiet understanding, every silent support. The tortoise's wise gaze met his, and in that moment, their bond transcended the physical realm entirely.

The Tower's destruction reached its peak. Stones flew upward resembling reverse rain, each one containing reflected images of London - both the real city and its twisted Arcanum reflection. The storm outside reached a crescendo, lightning forming a cage of electric fire around the chamber. Reality itself conveyed holding its breath, waiting to see which way it would fall.

In that moment of ultimate chaos, Lukas felt an odd sense of peace. He looked down at Tonto one last time, seeing in those knowing eyes the same determination that now filled his heart.

The cards in his hands began to glow with an inner light that had nothing to do with Arcanum's power. Each one resonated with truth - not the abstract concept of Truth, but his truth, earned through pain and joy and choice. Peter's puppets recoiled from this light, their corrupted forms unable to bear its simple honesty.

"This ends now," Lukas declared, raising the final card - The Tower. Its power spread outward in expanding rings of pure reality, pushing back against Peter's corruption. Where it touched the twisted stones, they remembered their true nature. Where it met the storm, the clouds parted to reveal true stars beyond.

The Tower's light reached the corrupted Arcana, and one by one, they began to transform. The masks of archetypes cracked and fell away, revealing the human faces beneath. In front of Lukas, Sarah gasped as Justice's balanced aura crumbled from her features, her eyes clearing of alien influence. As Lukas drew the Judgement card, its clarion call pierced through the chaos, and to his right, Mike stumbled as the Fool's garb melted away, leaving him in ordinary clothes, looking confused and disoriented.

"What..." Sarah stared at her hands, no longer surrounded by the scales' energy but ordinary, human fingers. "What's happening?"

"We've broken through," Lukas said, helping her to her feet. "This is just the beginning."

The Tower of London was fully collapsing now, not just in the chaotic anti-gravity of Arcanum, but as a symbol of false structures crumbling. Each stone that fell conveyed taking with it a piece of Peter's power. The very air became clearer, as if a film had been wiped from reality's lens.

A howl of rage and anguish tore through the chamber—Peter's true voice, stripped of artifice. For a moment, Lukas saw him clearly—not as the Devil, not as a monster, but as a man consumed by his own creations, trapped in a prison of his own making. Their eyes met across the disintegrating chamber, and in that brief connection, Lukas felt an unexpected empathy. There but for fortune might he have gone himself.

"This isn't over," Peter's voice cracked with emotion—fury, yes, but also a profound loss. His form flickered and destabilised, no longer the commanding presence it had been. "You've broken one tower, but Arcanum has many fortresses." He gestured weakly at the collapsing structure around them, his movements lacking their former fluid confidence. "Do you think this victory means anything? You've barely begun to understand what you're facing!"

The ceiling gave way completely, revealing not ordinary sky but a vast celestial panorama unlike anything Lukas had ever seen— constellations in configurations beyond conventional understanding, stars that pulsed with conscious light, cosmic bodies moving in deliberate arrangements that suggested purpose rather than orbital mechanics. For a moment, the entire group stood transfixed by the revelation above.

"The stars," whispered Sarah, her voice filled with wonder rather than fear. "They're... watching us."

"The true architects," Peter said, his voice suddenly subdued. He was fading now, his physical form becoming translucent, the edges of his being fraying resembling worn fabric. Lukas could sense the genuine depletion of Peter's power, his essence damaged and diminished by the battle. This wasn't merely a strategic withdrawal but a necessary retreat born of weakness. "Above my reach. Beyond your comprehension." A bitter smile crossed his face. "Ask your tortoise. He's older than he looks."

With that enigmatic statement, Peter vanished—his form dissolving into wisps of fading shadow. His departure left a silence that felt almost deafening after the chaos of battle.

Tonto pressed against Lukas's foot, his knowing eyes fixed on the celestial display above. For the first time, Lukas noticed arrangements on the tortoise's shell that conveyed mirroring the constellations overhead—subtle geometric markings that had always been there but somehow never registered in his awareness until now.

"We need to move," Mike said, rubbing his temples as if waking from a deep sleep. "This place isn't stable."

Lukas nodded, gathering his cards. "The Tower has fallen, but our journey continues." He looked at his freed friends, seeing the confusion and determination mingling on their faces. "Peter's retreated, wounded and weakened, but Arcanum still needs healing. And now we know there's something larger at work here—something even he answers to."

They made their way down through the crumbling Tower, following Tonto's confident lead. The tortoise moved with purpose, each step leaving a faint trail of starlight that reflected the celestial bodies now visible above. The building's interior had changed—no longer a nightmare of geometric impossibilities, but a ruin filled with relics of power. As they descended, Lukas noticed books, crystals, and artefacts that conveyed calling to him, knowledge waiting to be recovered.

Outside, Arcanum was transforming. The perpetual twilight had shifted—not to daylight, but to a true night sky filled with stars whose arrangements told stories Lukas somehow felt he should recognise. The Thames flowed normally again, its waters reflecting the celestial panorama above. London—not the London of his memory, but Arcanum's version—spread out before them, changed but still magical.

"What now?" Sarah asked, standing beside him at the Tower's base. Above them, the structure continued its symbolic collapse, each falling stone representing another false belief shattered, another deception revealed.

"Now we learn what the stars are trying to tell us," Lukas replied, looking up at the cosmic display. "This was never about escaping Arcanum. It's about understanding why we're here."

Tonto made a sound of agreement, his wise eyes reflecting pinpricks of starlight. The tortoise conveyed more alive, more present than ever before, as if the celestial revelation had awakened something within him as well.

As they walked away from the Tower's ruins, Lukas felt the cards in his pocket grow warm against his thigh, their magic evolving rather than fading. Arcanum had changed tonight, and so had he. The battle had been significant, but it was clear now that it was merely one chapter in a much longer story.

Behind them, the Tower of London continued its symbolic destruction in the starlight, each crumbling stone revealing more of the true sky above. Ahead lay a city transformed—not restored to normal, but elevated to something truer than it had been before. The ravens circled overhead, their calls now forming arrangements that matched the movements of the stars.

Lukas glanced back one last time before moving forward. The Tower conveyed winking at him, a flash of light from a window that couldn't possibly reflect the stars from that angle. A reminder that in Arcanum, nothing was ever quite as it seemed, and that some revelations were still waiting to be discovered.

With Tonto at his side and his freed friends behind him, he turned toward the city beneath the watching stars, ready for whatever would come next.

11

A Star In The Storm

Lukas sat on the fountain's edge in Trafalgar Square, the battle's aftermath etched on his face akin to new lines of wisdom. Above him, the sky remained that peculiar shade of twilight purple that never fully darkened or brightened. The great stone lions of Nelson's Column stood vigilant, timeless guardians of a city now in flux.

In the distance, where the Tower of London had stood just hours before, there was now a shimmering void—a wound in reality itself, edges ragged and pulsing with remnant energies. The Tower's collapse had changed everything. Its destruction had weakened Peter's control over Arcanum but had also destabilised the very fabric of this realm. The air felt thinner somehow, reality less certain. Occasionally, the stone beneath Lukas's feet would turn momentarily transparent, revealing glimpses of the ordinary Trafalgar Square in London proper— as if the boundary between worlds had grown permeable.

Around him, his companions remained in their Arcana forms, though those too appeared less stable now. Sarah still radiated Justice's otherworldly authority, but it flickered comparable to a candle in wind. Mike moved with The Fool's extraordinary grace, but occasionally stumbled as if remembering human limitations.

"What happens now?" Chloe asked, her form as one half of The Lovers occasionally merging with and separating from David's in a disorienting visual echo. The pair had joined Lukas's group after escaping their own ordeal in the Arcanum realm, their unique connection as The Lovers proving essential to their survival. "Is it over? Have we won?"

"Not yet," Lukas said, his voice carrying the newfound certainty that had come with embracing his role in this strange drama. "The Tower's fall was just one battle. Peter is wounded, but Arcanum still exists."

As if in confirmation of his words, a tremor ran through the square's surface, causing fracture lines to appear briefly before healing themselves. In the distance, buildings rearranged themselves with bewildering fluidity, streets folded like origami, and the purple sky rippled as if disturbed by unseen stones.

Tonto shifted in Lukas's arms, the tortoise's wisdom-filled eyes focusing on something approaching. Lukas turned to find three figures moving across the square, their forms so radiant that looking directly at them was almost painful. They moved in perfect synchronicity, though each emanated a distinctly different quality of light.

The first glowed with silver luminescence, her form constellation-like, with points of brilliant light connected by delicate filaments of energy. Her eyes were twin novas, compassionate but alien. The second figure shone with cool, reflective radiance, her curved form suggesting the waxing moon, her face half-hidden in perpetual shadow despite the light she emanated. The third blazed with golden intensity, his perfectly circular countenance too bright to observe directly, waves of heat and enlightenment pouring from him in palpable waves.

The Star. The Moon. The Sun.

"The highest Arcana," Mike whispered, instinctively dropping into a reverent bow. "The celestials."

Unlike the other Arcana, the godlike entities of Arcanum itself existed beyond Peter's darkening influence, neither controlled nor diminished by his power over the realm. Yet they rarely intervened directly, bound by age-old laws of balance that prevented them from simply overruling Peter's authority. Their power was cosmic but constrained by rules even they must obey—until the Tower's fall had created an opening for their appearance.

The Star spoke first, her voice reminiscent of distant wind chimes. "The Tower's fall was necessary. That which is built on false premises must eventually collapse."

"What was false about it?" Lukas asked, meeting that nova gaze despite the discomfort. "The Tower seemed real enough when we were fighting inside it."

The Moon laughed, a sound evocative of silver bells underwater. "Reality and perception are lovers who never quite embrace. What seems most solid is often most illusory."

The Sun's voice boomed with warming clarity: "The Tower was Peter's attempt to separate what cannot be divided. Arcanum is not apart from your London; it is your London, perceived through unclouded eyes."

Lukas frowned, trying to grasp the concept. "You're saying Arcanum and London are the same place? That's impossible. London doesn't have buildings that defy physics or streets that rearrange themselves or—"

"Doesn't it?" The Star moved closer, her constellation form shifting with each step. "Your London is constantly changing. Buildings rise and fall. Streets are renamed, re-routed. The Thames itself has been redirected by human will over centuries. The only difference is the speed at which change occurs and whether you can perceive the forces causing it."

The Moon drifted to the edge of the fountain, gesturing toward the void where the Tower had stood. "Peter's error was attempting to create a realm entirely separate from the world, a perfect Arcanum untouched by London's constraints. But such separation is impossible. One cannot exist without the other, just as I cannot exist without reflecting the Sun's light."

"Our perception shapes reality," Lukas said slowly, beginning to understand. "So Arcanum is London seen through a different... lens?"

"Not quite," the Sun corrected, his brightness momentarily dimming to allow Lukas to look directly at him. "Arcanum is London with its hidden truths made visible. The archetype beneath the ordinary. The essence behind the form."

Sarah stepped forward, Justice's sword materialising briefly in her hand before flickering out of existence. "Then why has Peter worked so hard to keep them separate? Why the battle at the Tower?"

The celestial trio exchanged glances, a silent communication passing between them. Finally, the Star answered: "Peter is ancient. He has witnessed cycles of revelation and concealment across millennia. Each age brings humans closer to perceiving the archetypal realms that underlie their reality, and each time, fear drives them to rebuild the walls between worlds."

"He believes he protects humanity," the Moon added, her half-hidden face revealing a sad smile. "He thinks your minds too fragile to perceive reality's true nature without the buffer of ordinary perception."

Before anyone could respond, a painful distortion rippled through Arcanum. The stone beneath their feet momentarily dissolved into ordinary concrete before reassembling itself. Buildings in the distance melted and reformed. The sky thinned, revealing glimpses of ordinary blue.

"He comes," the Moon whispered, turning toward the source of the disturbance.

From the direction of the Tower's void emerged a figure Lukas recognised immediately—Peter, now wearing James's face but imperfectly now. The handsome features flickered and wavered, occasionally revealing glimpses of something primordial and wounded beneath. He moved with a limp, one arm cradled against his chest, trailing iridescent blue-black droplets that shimmered reminiscent of oil.

Despite his injured state, power still radiated from him in waves of distortion. Each step he took stabilised the fluctuating reality around them, forcing Arcanum back into solid existence.

"Interesting company you keep, Lukas," Peter called, his voice alternating between James's familiar tones and something older, deeper. "The celestials rarely descend to involve themselves directly. I'm almost flattered."

"The Tower is gone," Lukas said, surprised by the steadiness in his own voice. "Your hold on Arcanum is weakening."

Peter laughed, the sound causing painful ripples in the air. "The Tower was just one manifestation. Arcanum existed before it and will continue long after." His gaze swept over Lukas's companions before settling on the celestial trio. "Though perhaps not in the form these three would prefer."

"You misunderstand our purpose," the Star said gently. "We do not seek Arcanum's destruction."

"Only its truth," added the Moon.

"And freedom for those within it," the Sun concluded.

Peter's borrowed face contorted with genuine pain—emotional rather than physical. "Freedom? You speak of freedom while guiding them to unravel the very realm that gives them form?" He gestured toward Sarah, Mike, and the others. "Without Arcanum, they return to being merely human. With it, they are archetypal. Transcendent."

The celestials remained unmoved by his argument, their light steady and impartial. Peter's expression hardened as he turned his attention back to Lukas.

"You still don't understand what you're destroying," he said, voice softening to sound painfully reminiscent of James's most intimate tone. "What you could help preserve, enhance. You belong here, Lukas, whether you know it yet or not."

The words stirred something in Lukas—a recognition, a longing. Part of him had indeed found a belonging in Arcanum that he'd never quite experienced in ordinary London. Here, configurations made sense. Symbols had power. Meaning wasn't constantly undermined by irony or distraction.

Sensing his hesitation, Peter took a step closer, his form stabilising to look more completely like James. "You've glimpsed only the surface. There are depths to Arcanum that would answer every question you've ever had about meaning, about purpose. About love."

Tonto stirred in Lukas's arms, the tortoise's knowing stare fixing on him with quiet warning. The celestials too appeared to be waiting, observing his response without interfering.

"I've seen enough to know that your version of Arcanum is built on control, not truth," Lukas finally said. "You're not preserving it; you're constraining it to your vision alone."

Peter's face flickered between James's features and something else—something with eyes that had witnessed centuries. "My vision has sustained it for millennia! What would you have instead? Chaos? The merging of worlds until neither has meaning or structure?"

"Perhaps what lies between total separation and complete merger," Lukas suggested. "A balance where Arcanum and London inform each other without consuming each other."

The celestials stirred at this, their light brightening in what might have been approval.

"Impossible," Peter snapped, though doubt had crept into his voice. "The human mind cannot hold both realities simultaneously without breaking. I've seen it happen countless times across centuries."

"Perhaps in the past," the Star interjected. "But consciousness evolves. What was unimaginable becomes possible. What was hidden becomes visible."

"Each age carries its own potential," agreed the Moon.

"And this age may finally be ready for the veils to thin," completed the Sun.

Peter stared at them, primordial eyes visible through the mask of James's face. For a moment, Lukas glimpsed something beyond the adversarial role Peter had assumed—a weariness, a loneliness, the burden of ages spent maintaining boundaries that perhaps no longer needed to exist.

Another tremor ran through Arcanum, stronger than before. The stone beneath them cracked audibly, and in the distance, buildings began to lose definition, their edges blurring reminiscent of watercolours in rain.

"It's becoming critical," Peter said, urgency replacing anger. "Without the Tower's stabilising influence, Arcanum and London are bleeding into each other too quickly. If the process isn't controlled, both realms could be irreparably damaged."

"What happens if they merge completely?" Lukas asked, looking to the celestials for answers.

The Star's constellation form flickered. "Unknown. Such a merger has not occurred in living memory."

"It would be neither destruction nor salvation," the Moon added cryptically. "But transformation."

"For better or worse depends on how it happens," the Sun concluded. "Violent collision or harmonious integration."

Peter extended a hand toward Lukas, blood—that strange iridescent blue-black—still seeping from his wounded arm. "Help me stabilise it. You've proven yourself capable of working with Arcanum's energies. Together, we can manage the transition, maintain the necessary boundaries."

The offer was tempting. Despite everything, Lukas couldn't help but feel drawn to the idea of helping preserve this remarkable realm, of having a hand in shaping something so profound. But Tonto shifted in his arms again, drawing his attention. The tortoise's timeless gaze held a warning—not against action, but against haste. Some decisions shouldn't be made in the heat of crisis.

"First, I need to understand more," Lukas said finally. "About Arcanum. About how it relates to London. About what it means for everyone involved." He nodded toward his companions, who watched the exchange with varying degrees of confusion and concern.

Peter's expression darkened. "Understanding can wait. Action must come now, while there's still—"

"No," Lukas interrupted firmly. "Understanding must come first. That's where you've always been wrong, Peter. You act without explaining, control without consulting, decide without sharing your knowledge."

Before Peter could respond, silver light bathed them all as the Star moved forward. "The young one is right," she said, her voice reminiscent of distant music. "Knowledge must precede action. And there is much he still needs to learn."

"Beginning with the truth about perception," added the Moon, moving toward the fountain. Her silvery form reflected in the water's surface as she gestured for Lukas to look down. "Let this show you what has been hidden."

The fountain's pool shimmered, its reflective surface transforming into images of times past and futures possible.

"And the secret history of the realms," completed the Sun.

The celestial trio surrounded Lukas, their light creating a protective circle that excluded Peter. The wounded ancient took a step back, frustration evident on his borrowed features.

"There isn't time for philosophical discussions," he warned. "Arcanum is destabilising. Without immediate intervention—"

"Time moves differently in the presence of the celestials," the Star informed Lukas, ignoring Peter's protest. "What seems moments to him will give us hours to share what you need to know."

"Come," the Moon beckoned, her reflection in the fountain deepening, becoming a window to other times and places. "Let us show you the truth…"

"Yes", the Sun added. "The truth beyond the Tower."

Lukas hesitated, looking toward his companions who remained outside the circle of celestial light. Sarah nodded encouragingly, Mike gave a thumbs-up, and Chloe and David smiled in unison.

"We'll be fine," Sarah assured him. "This is your journey to make."

Tonto squirmed in Lukas's arms, clearly indicating he wished to accompany him into the celestial light. Taking a deep breath, Lukas stepped forward with the tortoise, allowing the radiance of the Star, Moon, and Sun to envelop them completely.

The last thing he saw before the light became all-encompassing was Peter's face—James's features sliding away completely to reveal what lay beneath: a man neither young nor old, with eyes that had witnessed the rise and fall of civilisations, whose expression held not malice but a complex mixture of fear, resignation, and something that might almost have been hope.

From the wounded void where the Tower had stood, something stirred—neither light nor darkness but the possibility of both, watching and waiting for the moment when choice would become destiny.

12

The Moon's Reflection

In the shimmering light, the cascading fountains at the heart of London's grandest square subsided, their chaotic spray giving way as the waters became calm and still. Stone lions watched impassively from their plinths, venerable guardians bearing witness to the transformation unfolding below the towering column that pierced the twilight sky. The Moon's reflection bathed in the mirrored surface, her luminescence both familiar and alien. She beckoned Lukas forward with an elegant gesture, and as she did so, scenes of the river appeared in a montage of things yet to come—visions dancing across the water's tranquil face.

"All roads lead back to the river," she explained, her voice carrying that disembodied chorus of whispers that accompanied her every word. "The Thames has always been a boundary between worlds—a place of transition. If there is a way for you to return home safely, we will find it there."

Her eyes, pools of primeval light, fixed on Lukas with sombre knowing. "That said... the way home for you is not so clear. Peter will try and keep you within Arcanum by any means—you have a little further to go and there's still a lot to give, and lose."

As he watched, transfixed by the liquid prophecy, one by one, his guides began to vanish from the visions. The High Priestess smiled sadly as her form blurred, the arcane tattoos that had marked her power fading reminiscent of smoke signals in a storm. The Hermit, who had taught him so much about Arcanum's deepest mysteries, dissolved mid-sentence, his final wisdom lost to the void.

Lukas suddenly realised what was happening. "They're not just returning to their places," he said with dawning understanding. "Everything is shifting—Arcanum itself is being rewritten."

"There," he pointed to a rippling section of air where colours shifted resembling oil on water. "That's a nodal point—where the world's restructuring itself." Rather than simply fleeing chaos, he was mapping it, understanding it. "If we time it right, we can use the collapse to find our way home."

Suddenly there was a startled cry behind him, and momentarily the spell was broken, scenes fractured and dissolved and the light was gone. He turned to see Sarah begin to fade before his eyes. Her regal bearing, which had commanded such authority throughout his journey, dissolved akin to morning mist. The scales and sword she carried crumbled into stardust, scattering on a spectral wind that howled with voices from both worlds. Gone was the precision and fairness that had characterised her presence throughout his journey, her unwavering commitment to balance now making perfect sense in light of her Justice aspect.

"Sarah!" Lukas cried out, reaching for her desperately. "Where are you going?"

"Do not fear for her," The Moon's voice echoed reassuringly even as Sarah's presence dissipated. "She is safe in your world. The Arcana within is being pulled back, but your friend remains untouched in your reality."

As she faded, Lukas felt a disorienting pull in his own body—as though some essential quality was being drawn from him. His vision briefly doubled, and he tasted chalk in his mouth. He realised the scenes in the fountain had been a prediction of what was to follow—The High Priestess, The Hermit and now Sarah. Each Arcanum resident who departed took with them a small fragment of the magic sustaining this place, and with each loss, the fundamental laws binding this reality grew more tenuous.

"The boundaries dissolve," The Moon's light pulsed urgently. "We are being pulled back. Those of us borrowed from your world must retreat... or be lost forever between realities."

"We must hurry," The Moon whispered, with a voice that carried a disembodied chorus of sorrow. Her manifestation shimmered violently, the edges of her presence becoming translucent, stars visible through her increasingly ethereal essence. "The veil between worlds grows dangerously thin. Those of Arcanum must return... or risk absolute oblivion."

The Moon led their procession down the Strand, away from Trafalgar Square and turned toward the Thames. Her silvery form illuminated the path ahead through Arcanum's increasingly unstable landscape.

The journey felt both urgent and dreamlike as buildings around them flickered between solidity and translucence. Streets that should have been straight now curved beyond natural explanation, sometimes doubling back on themselves. Yet the Moon guided them unerringly, following a path that appeared to exist more in concept than in physical space.

As they journeyed toward the river, Lukas watched in silent dismay as his companions began to succumb to Arcanum's dissolution. One by one, his guides began to vanish from the procession, their essences dispersing into the fractured atmosphere resembling stardust caught in cosmic winds.

Mike was the first to fade, but true to The Fool's nature, his departure defied the solemn sequence. As the edges of his form began to blur, he caught Lukas's eye with a knowing grin. With deliberate grace, he executed an elaborate pirouette at the edge of their path, spinning faster until his outline smeared into a streak of joyful colour. With a final, extraordinary step, he danced sideways into a shadow that conveyed far too shallow to contain him—yet swallowed him completely. His laughter remained a moment longer than his image, hanging in the air reminiscent of the final notes of a beloved song.

Finally, The Star began to dim. Lukas watched with an ache in his chest as her luminescence—which had offered such steady hope throughout his darkest moments—faltered and waned. The warm certainty of her guidance, which had been his most reliable beacon in Arcanum's shifting reality, receded to a distant pinpoint before blinking out completely.

Each disappearance tore a wound in the fabric of Arcanum itself—rents in reality through which nothingness seeped akin to groundwater. Lukas felt each departure as a physical hollowing, as though essential pieces of himself were being carved away along with his guides.

As they reached the Embankment, the full impact of Arcanum's deterioration became apparent. The grand stone balustrade that normally lined the river was intact in some sections but completely missing in others, revealing vertigo-inducing drops to the churning waters below. Lukas approached one of the solid sections and leaned against the stone wall, gazing eastward where Tower Bridge stood silhouetted against the strange twilight. In the distance, where the Tower of London should have been, he could make out tattered flags fluttering above the shimmering void that had replaced the time-worn fortress.

The moonlight painted the Thames with an unsettling, argent glow. It wasn't the familiar, comforting silver of Lukas's London, but a fractured, almost sentient light that conveyed breathing—

THE MOON'S REFLECTION

expanding and contracting with a rhythm that made his chest tighten in sympathetic response. The river below moved with extraordinary contradiction, flowing in two directions at once—one current rushing towards the sea with familiar urgency, while another surged inland, thick with a presence that felt conscious, evaluating, alien. Where the flows collided, Lukas felt a vertigo so profound he had to look away—time itself appeared wounded there, moments stretching until they became toffee-like and malleable, then compressing violently into singularities of experience so dense they left after-images on his consciousness.

Lukas reached for a nearby railing, but his hand passed through the iron resembling smoke. He felt neither solid matter nor complete emptiness, but rather a resistance reminiscent of moving through honey, accompanied by a faint electric tingle that travelled up his arm and settled uncomfortably in his chest. The very structures of Arcanum were degrading, transforming from solid matter into memory. Along the embankment, Victorian lampposts twisted into extraordinary shapes, their light fracturing into prismatic shards that hung suspended in the air.

Lukas turned to The Moon. "Let me help you," he said, reaching toward her dissolving form.

He placed his hands on either side of her increasingly transparent face. Drawing on the instinct that had guided him through Arcanum, he visualised her form stabilising. The Moon's features solidified momentarily, a familiar smile breaking through the cosmic mask.

"No one has ever tried to anchor us before," she whispered, surprise evident in her voice. "Always taking, never giving..."

Tonto pressed against Lukas's ankle, nudging him towards a section of the bank that still maintained some solidity. The tortoise's all-seeing eyes reflected the extraordinary moonlight, holding millennia of wisdom in their depths. But even Tonto's movements appeared laboured now, as if the very air was becoming gelatinous with collapsing realities.

Lukas faced a choice: follow the paths of dissolution where navigation conveyed safest, or strike out across a more chaotic section where reality itself was writing and rewriting with dizzying speed. The safe path would take longer, perhaps too long as the boundaries between worlds healed. The dangerous path offered directness but risked being caught in reality's reconstruction.

"Sometimes the most challenging story leads to the most truthful resolution," he said with deliberate certainty. Lukas stepped onto the chaotic path, Tonto following with time-worn trust.

Panic clawed at Lukas's chest as the Thames roared beneath them, its dual flow creating interference waves that bent light and shadow into extraordinary arrangements. Each wave held fragments of both worlds—London's gritty reality and Arcanum's fading wonder colliding in a spray of temporal chaos.

"Beware the undertow," The Moon warned, her form growing increasingly transparent. Around her, reality shimmered evocative of heat waves over asphalt, but in precise forms that resembled pages of text with words rearranging themselves. "The river flows both ways now—towards your past, towards the idea of your future. Choose your crossing carefully."

She gestured to the water, where Lukas now saw distinct currents marked by subtle differences in colour and movement. One flowed with the familiar muddy brown of Thames water, carrying the scent of clay and industry—the path back to ordinary London. Another current flowed milky white, shimmering with possibilities, smelling of ozone and potential—leading deeper into the heart of Arcanum. Where these currents met, dangerous eddies formed, swirling with hypnotic motions.

"One wrong step and you'll be trapped between moments," she continued, her voice echoing strangely as her form grew fainter.

THE MOON'S REFLECTION

"Forever caught in the space between decisions."

As the Moon's silvery radiance began to dim, retreating into the deepening shadows of Arcanum's increasingly unstable reality, her final warning came as barely a whisper: "Time is fluid here, Lukas. You might walk into yesterday... or a tomorrow that never arrives..."

Then she too was gone, leaving Lukas and Tonto alone on the rapidly dissolving riverbank. The journey home, it appeared, would require navigating not just space, but the treacherous currents of time itself.

Instead of waiting for the next guide or revelation, Lukas knelt beside Tonto. "We've been following others' paths since we arrived," he said quietly. "But maybe that was never the point. Maybe we need to create our own."

Drawing upon everything he'd learned about Arcanum's nature, Lukas took a deep breath and began to speak in a clear, resonant voice—telling a story of return, of homecoming, of finding one's true path. It wasn't a story he'd crafted for someone else this time, but his own narrative, too personal to have shared professionally. As the words vibrated through the air, small pockets of stability formed in the chaos around them, stepping stones of solid reality amid the dissolving landscape.

"Stories create structure," he realised aloud. "And structure is what we need now."

The fractured moonlight scattered across the Thames, each shard a mirror reflecting a different possible reality. Lukas stood at the edge of the bridge, Tonto's reliable weight against his feet, as a figure coalesced from the silvery mist. Peter had chosen James's face again, but this time, the borrowed features conveyed strained—beautiful, yes, but with an underlying tension that suggested maintaining the disguise required increasing effort. Occasionally, when he thought Lukas wasn't looking, the mask slipped, revealing flashes of another face beneath—not monstrous as Lukas might have expected, but tired, almost desperately lonely, with eyes that had witnessed epochs pass resembling seasons.

"You look exhausted, love," Peter murmured, moving closer. The illusion faltered slightly—James's crooked smile appeared, but a microsecond too late after the words, as if the synchronisation was breaking down. The eyes crinkled correctly, but held an unfamiliar desperation. Even the small childhood accident scar appeared sharper, newer somehow. "I don't think you understand what I'm truly offering, Lukas. Not just power or escape, but belonging. Connection." His voice shifted subtly, no longer perfectly mimicking James but taking on its own distinctive timbre. "I was a mathematician too, once. I created equations that tried to model consciousness itself. When they labelled me mad, I found my way here—where understanding doesn't need to be constrained by their arbitrary rules." He gestured around them, and for a moment, Arcanum's beauty outshone its menace. "Here, you could be extraordinary. Here, we could be extraordinary together."

Tonto nudged Lukas's foot, but even the tortoise's grounding presence couldn't entirely dispel the seductive power radiating from the tempter. Peter gestured at the transformed cityscape, and the air shimmered with possibilities, each one a carefully crafted lure designed to ensnare desire itself. In his role as eternal adversary, he offered not crude corruption but the more insidious temptation of dreams fulfilled without true cost—the most primordial deception in existence.

Reality split into shards, each reflecting a different promise. In one, Lukas saw himself in a Victorian study lined with books that whispered age-old secrets, respected and feared by both mortal and magical beings. In another, he crafted lines so powerful they would appear to almost reshape reality itself, the Thames rising to the rhythms of his words. But the most dangerous vision showed quiet evenings in a moonlit garden, James by his side, their love unmarked by mundane concerns or painful partings.

THE MOON'S REFLECTION

"Think of what you're returning to," Peter pressed, his voice wrapping around Lukas's deepest doubts akin to silk. As he spoke, there was something primeval and practised in his technique—the oldest game of temptation played across countless souls throughout time. "Mortgage payments. Rain-soaked commutes. Watching James pull away again, buried in work and ambition, checking his phone during your conversations, missing the subtle meanings you've woven into each careful phrase." He paused, and when he spoke again, the words carried a weight of personal experience. "Is it worth it, Lukas? Is perfect understanding worth the isolation it brings? I've stood where you stand now—torn between worlds, between connection and comprehension. They can never fully understand what you've seen, what you've become. Even if you try to explain, the words will sound like madness to them." A deep sorrow passed across his features, momentarily genuine. "I chose understanding. I chose to see reality as it truly is, and I've been alone ever since. Until now. Until you."

The bridge groaned beneath them, its steel and stone fighting against Arcanum's dissolution. To the north, London lay cloaked in ordinary shadow, its familiar streets promising nothing but routine and limitation. To the south, Arcanum glittered with intoxicating potential, despite its unravelling reality. The Thames, flowing in both directions, reflected both choices in its chaotic surface.

"You would choose a world without him?" said Peter, looking down at Tonto. "A mundane existence without magic?"

Lukas smiled through his tears, a genuine, heartfelt smile that reached his eyes. "There's magic in every world. In every moment. Tonto showed me that. His love wasn't about lasting forever—it was about being real. Being true."

As Lukas spoke, his voice gained a resonant quality that matched and then overwhelmed Peter's harmonic complexity. Where Peter's voice combined existing sounds, Lukas's words appeared to create new frequencies—not by supernatural power but through the authentic emotion behind them. This wasn't magic as Peter understood it, but something more fundamental that existed before and beyond Arcanum's distortions.

"I've spent my life crafting narratives for others," Lukas continued, his voice steady and clear. "I've always been a storyteller at heart. But I'm not manufacturing truth. I'm finding it—revealing it. And the story I need to tell now is my own."

Peter's borrowed face flickered with a complex mix of emotions—admiration, envy, and something akin to grief. "You really think you can go back to that world and bring any of this with you? They'll never believe you. Never understand."

"Perhaps not," Lukas acknowledged. "But I don't need them to believe in Arcanum to believe in possibility. In wonder."

The storm unleashed its full fury then, a vortex of wind and water threatening to tear Arcanum apart at its seams. Lukas clung to a lamppost that bent akin to rubber, while the Thames raged below, a serpent of shadow and extraordinary currents. Tonto pressed against his ankle with urgent determination, an anchor in the chaos.

"Hold on, old friend!" Lukas yelled, his words instantly swallowed by the tempest. "We've come too far to lose each other now!"

A massive wave crashed against the bridge, but instead of falling away, it hung suspended, crystallising into forms that rotated through dimensions that shouldn't exist before shattering into shards that flew upward into the storm. Reality itself was unravelling. Peter's laughter echoed from everywhere and nowhere, wearing James's voice akin to an ill-fitting mask.

In that moment of crisis, Tonto's weight shifted precariously. The tortoise, for one heart-stopping moment, began to be dragged away on a current of air that defied gravity. Without hesitation, Lukas released his grip on the lamppost and lunged, catching Tonto in his arms as they both fell to the slick cobbles.

"I've got you," he gasped, holding the tortoise close, the shell warm against his chest. The contact produced a momentary resonance—a perfect harmony that rang clearly through the chaos—as their energies aligned. Tonto's venerable eyes held an unwavering trust that cut through all of Peter's illusions.

They scrambled for shelter under an archway that breathed akin to a living thing, expanding and contracting with each gust of wind. The stones whispered secrets in forgotten languages, their voices blending with the roar of the storm into an eldritch symphony.

Vertigo struck as Lukas watched the river's extraordinary convergence, where the swirling vortex reached toward churning clouds in shades of violet and emerald never seen in nature. Peter's voice came from everywhere, wearing a thousand familiar faces, offering a thousand perfect lives.

"Which way home, Tonto?" Lukas whispered, raw with fear and wonder.

The tortoise extended his neck, pointing with slow deliberation toward a pocket of darkness that appeared to swallow all light around it. In that void, Lukas caught glimpses of his ordinary London—not perfect, not magical, but real. The absence of magic had its own specific quality—not emptiness but a different kind of fullness, characterised by consistency rather than wonder. That steadiness called to something deep within him, a longing for terra-firma after too long at sea.

Lightning struck, but instead of illuminating, it cast moving shadows that operated independently of light. In that fractured moment, Lukas saw shadows multiply and divide, each showing a possible path—some leading home, some leading to eternal entrapment in Arcanum's dying dream.

"We have to move now," Lukas decided, his voice steady despite his fear.

But as he stepped forward, a violent gust threatened to tear Tonto from his arms. He tightened his grip on the rough shell, feeling its weight flicker between heavy and light as reality continued to fold in on itself.

Muscles straining, they pressed on as the world bent around them. Each step was akin to wading through treacle, the air thick with dissolving magic. Cobblestones ahead folded upward resembling pages in a closing book, revealing glimpses of the void beneath. Buildings that had merely been unstable before now collapsed entirely into conceptual sketches of themselves—mere outlines filled with swirling possibility rather than solid matter. Lukas skirted the edge, feeling Tonto push his head against his chest in silent encouragement.

"Together," Lukas promised, voice hoarse. "Whatever happens... we stay together."

The storm reached its crescendo, and for a long, extraordinary moment, they were suspended in a wall of water, frozen at the heart of chaos. Through the swirl, Lukas watched buildings bend and twist, architecture surrendering to unfathomable forces.

Then the bubble burst, and they fell once more into the maelstrom. But this time, something had changed. Peter's voice had lost its power, its promises hollow against the simple truth of Tonto's unwavering presence.

Their clothes were soaked, but the water ran upward instead of down. Tonto's shell glistened with droplets that formed sacred geometries before dissipating into steam. Together, they pressed on through the storm, each step a declaration of will against the dying magic of Arcanum.

They moved forward, their bond forged across fractured worlds becoming something unbreakable—stronger than temptation, truer than illusion, more magical than all of Arcanum's fading wonders.

As reality twisted and time folded around them, Lukas finally understood. The real magic had never been in the cards or the transformed city or Peter's promises. It had been there all along, in the quiet courage of taking one more step, in the choice to hold on when letting go would be easier, in the love that asked for nothing but offered everything. And perhaps most importantly, in the power of stories—not to deceive, but to reveal truth, to create bridges between worlds, between people.

And together, they walked into darkness, toward home.

13

The Sun Rises

The air lay still, a morning breath held captive inside Arcanum's Kennington Park. The usual chaotic symphony of unnatural angles and shimmering distortions had fallen silent, replaced by an eerie stillness. Above, frost-limned windows caught the pearl-grey dawn, their reflections twisting into delicate fractals that conveyed stories of their own. One of the Georgian terraces leaned at an almost imperceptible angle, just enough to make the reflections in its windows stretch and warp the world within.

Lukas sat on a park bench that wavered precariously between existence and non-existence, his hand resting on the familiar, weathered shell of Tonto. Wreaths hung on doors at angles defying physics, their red berries glowing with an inner light that pulsed in time with some unheard celestial rhythm. The park was decorated comparable to Christmas in Arcanum's own peculiar way – icicles that grew upward instead of down, tinsel that moved akin to liquid silver in the still air fairy lights that appeared to illuminate spaces that didn't quite exist.

"Just us now, old friend," he murmured, his voice a fragile thread in the heavy silence. He scratched lightly at the spot behind Tonto's head, a gesture that usually elicited a contented shift from the timeless

THE SUN RISES

tortoise. Today there was nothing.

His fingers found the small notch in Tonto's shell—a perfect semicircle worn smooth with age. Lukas remembered the first time he'd noticed it, when they were fleeing The Magician's illusions. He'd asked about it during a rare moment of rest. Tonto had pressed against his hand with unusual insistence, as if to say some scars were memories worth keeping. That silent answer had sustained Lukas through their darkest moments in The Tower, had reminded him that imperfection often marked the most important experiences.

"Quite the journey, eh? Never thought I'd see the inside of a magic shop, let alone another dimension."

The square, at first glance, resembled a postcard of Georgian serenity. But familiarity was a deceptive mask in Arcanum. Iron railings curled in unnatural spirals, and the branches of plane trees traced mathematical equations too perfect to be natural against the pearl-grey sky.

Tonto's eyes, venerable wells of timeless wisdom, met Lukas's. They held a familiar knowing, a patient understanding that had guided him through countless perils. The tortoise shifted, pressing against Lukas's leg with unusual tenderness. A silent farewell.

"I'll miss this place, in a strange way," Lukas confessed, his voice barely a whisper. "Even with all its dangers. The way the buildings dance when they think no one's watching. The clouds that flow akin to water. The light that comes from nowhere and everywhere at once."

His mind wandered to their encounter with The Hermit, how Tonto had somehow communicated with the ancient figure in a language beyond words. The tortoise had positioned himself precisely between Lukas and danger, his shell catching moonlight in configurations that had momentarily confused Peter's servants. Not for the first time, Lukas wondered how many travellers Tonto had guided before him, how many souls had relied on those knowing eyes to navigate

Arcanum's treacherous beauty.

A single leaf, brittle and brown, skittered across the square, tracing a perfect Fibonacci spiral on the cobblestones. A design born of something far beyond the reach of any earthly soft breeze.

The silence deepened, heavy with unspoken goodbyes, with the weight of the journey's inevitable end. Tonto emitted a soft sound, a low rumble deep within his ageless frame, a sound that could have been a sigh or a contented hum. It drew Lukas's attention back to the tortoise. The usual golden glow that emanated from the intricate designs on his shell appeared dimmer now, flickering equivalent to candlelight in a dying breeze.

"You've been the best guide I could have asked for," Lukas said, his voice catching. He noticed the vibrant energy that usually pulsed beneath Tonto's shell appeared muted, comparable to stars fading at dawn. "I don't think I would have survived Peter's tricks without you."

He remembered their first escape from Peter, when Tonto had led him through what appeared to be a solid wall, somehow knowing exactly where reality thinned enough to pass through. Lukas had panicked, certain they were about to crash into unyielding stone, but Tonto had pressed firmly against his ankle, a silent command to trust.

The tortoise stilled. His head drooped slightly, his usually bright eyes clouding over with a film that wasn't quite sorrow but something deeper—acceptance, perhaps. The small claws of a partially extended leg lost their grip, falling limp against Lukas's trousers.

Above them, the church bells of Arcanum began to toll – not the familiar peals of London churches, but something deeper, more resonant, as if the very fabric of reality was chiming its own transformation.

Alarm shot through Lukas. He slid from the bench, kneeling beside his friend, his hand trembling as he reached out. "Tonto? What's wrong?"

The timeless creature's eyes met his once more, filled with a profound mixture of joy and a heart-wrenching certainty. Tonto's breathing became shallow, each inhale a gentle effort against the weight of centuries.

"No," Lukas whispered, gathering the tortoise gently into his arms. "Please, no. Not now. Not when we're so close to home."

He cradled Tonto against his chest, feeling the venerable shell beneath his fingers. It felt different somehow, lighter. As if the very essence that animated the creature, the magic that had allowed him to navigate the treacherous currents of Arcanum, was slowly dissolving—not into nothingness, but into something else, something that might continue in another form.

Lukas remembered that first meeting – Tonto on that little red stool outside Cassandra's shop, those knowing eyes fixing him with a gaze that somehow reminded him of his first music teacher, the one who'd taught him to hear the spaces between notes as carefully as the notes themselves. Tonto had guided him with that same silent wisdom, communicating volumes through the smallest shifts in posture, teaching Lukas to perceive arrangements and harmonies in Arcanum that would have otherwise remained invisible to him. Every nudge, every gentle pressure against his ankle had been a note in their unspoken duet, a composition written in trust and mutual understanding.

"Please," Lukas begged, his voice cracking. "I still need you. We haven't finished our journey."

The plea hung in the still air, unanswered. In the distance, Big Ben tolled backwards through time, each strike resonating with the weight of moments slipping away.

Tonto pressed his head against Lukas's hand one final time, a gesture of unconditional love and friendship. His timeless eyes, filled with centuries of wisdom, softened with acceptance that it was time to part, and the configurations on his shell, which had always appeared to shift and change unlike other living things, began to pulse with newfound intensity, as if gathering themselves for something momentous.

With a final, soft exhalation that conveyed the echoes of countless worlds, Tonto's physical form grew still. Yet the venerable designs beneath Lukas's fingers didn't simply fade—they intensified, becoming brighter, more distinct, as though preparing for something beyond mere ending.

The square plunged into an unfathomable silence, a stillness so profound it felt akin to the moment between heartbeats. The buildings appeared to bow inward, their unnatural angles twisting into curves of reverence. Even the ever-present shimmer of Arcanum's magic gathered itself, condensing around them comparable to dew preparing to transform.

Lukas cradled the ancient tortoise, tears streaming down his face, each drop a tiny burst of warmth against the cooling shell. Each tear captured and held the strange light of Arcanum, refracting it into miniature rainbows that danced across the venerable designs.

"I don't understand," Lukas whispered, his fingers tracing the intricate designs on Tonto's shell. Each groove felt akin to a story, a map of all the journeys they'd shared. It contained that same ineffable quality – information encoded in a language beyond words, yet somehow perfectly comprehensible to the heart.

As his fingers traced one particular swirling motif, a small section - no larger than a guitar pick—came loose in his hand. The piece appeared to have detached naturally along one of the shell's seams. Lukas stared at it in wonder, noticing how it continued to glow faintly with Arcanum's peculiar light. Without thinking, he carefully placed it in his shirt pocket, feeling an instinctive need to keep this small token of his extraordinary friend.

The morning light cast long shadows across the square, but these shadows behaved properly for the first time since he'd entered this

THE SUN RISES

realm. No dancing at the edges, no subtle movements when no one was watching. Just ordinary shadows marking ordinary time. Even the ambient sounds had changed, the ethereal overtones of Arcanum fading into the simpler acoustics of ordinary reality, as though the cosmic symphony was diminishing into a more limited tonal range.

"Thank you," he whispered, his words carrying the weight of all they had shared, all the unspoken understanding that had bound them together. "Thank you for everything."

As the last word left his lips, something extraordinary happened. A single snowflake appeared, materialising out of the still, grey air. It was unlike anything Lukas had ever seen in Arcanum. This realm was a place of uncanny skies and implausible geometry; snow, that purest expression of earthly winter, had never existed here.

This snowflake defied even the altered laws of this realm. Instead of falling, it drifted upwards from the ground, a delicate white feather ascending towards the pearl-grey sky. Then another followed, and another, until the air was filled with a silent, surreal ballet. Snowflakes rose from the cobblestones, from the bare branches of the plane trees, from the rooftops of the unimaginably angled buildings, all rising in a silent, reverent tribute.

It was as if the world itself was weeping in reverse, mourning the loss of this extraordinary being. Each ascending flake caught the light in ways defying natural laws, carrying fragments of memories within their crystalline structures – offering traces of all the lives Tonto had touched, all the travellers he had guided through Arcanum's treacherous paths.

Lukas remained kneeling in the gravity-defying snow, holding his friend, the weight of grief heavy on his shoulders. He understood that some endings were also beginnings, that love, even in farewell, possessed its own unique and potent magic.

Through his tears, he saw the configurations on Tonto's shell beginning to change—not fading comparable to paint washing away but transforming, rearranging themselves into new designs akin to stars forming fresh constellations.

The rising snow intensified, creating a vortex of white around Lukas and Tonto. The flakes danced in the air, catching the pale light and turning the square into a swirling nebula of transformation. Each snowflake conveyed a piece of Arcanum's magic within it, transforming the ordinary act of snowfall into something profound and sacred.

In the distance, church bells began to toll – real bells this time, their sound pure and unmistakably of the ordinary world. The border between realms was thinning, and through his tears, Lukas could see the familiar shapes of London beginning to emerge through Arcanum's shifting facade.

The upward-falling snow began to gather around them, creating ghostly columns of white that defied gravity. Each crystalline particle caught the light akin to a shard of memory, making the air shimmer with countless points of illumination. The cold beauty of it only emphasised the growing stillness in his arms.

A single flake broke from the arrangement, drifting up from Tonto's shell with deliberate slowness. As it passed through a shaft of morning light, it refracted the beam into a momentary spectrum. In that prismatic instant, Lukas saw everything – every step of their journey together, every silent communication, every moment of guidance and protection. He saw the strength Tonto had instilled in him, the courage he had unknowingly drawn from the timeless creature's unwavering presence.

"It wasn't about getting home, was it?" he said softly. "It was never about finding my way back to London. It was about understanding that love..." He paused as the gravity-defying snow swirled around them. "Love transcends all of this. Even magic. Even death."

The realisation settled over him comparable to the weight of all the ascending snow – gentle but unfathomable to ignore. Tonto had known

THE SUN RISES

from the beginning that this journey would end here, in this quiet square, with this final lesson. The greatest magic wasn't in the cards or in Arcanum's unnatural architecture – it was in the connections formed, the truths learned, the love shared.

In the corner of the square, a grandfather clock that hadn't been there moments before began to chime. Its face showed time moving in all directions at once, but its sound was pure and true. Each strike conveyed the weight of Tonto's final gift – the understanding that real magic existed in both worlds, in the simple act of loving despite knowing loss would come.

As the clock completed its mind-bending count, a small design on Tonto's shell—right where Lukas's tears had fallen—began to glow with quiet persistence. The design separated from the shell, hovering momentarily in the air as a luminous symbol before settling onto Lukas's palm. It burned cold for a moment before fading into his skin, leaving a faint mark akin to an ancient sigil—its meaning a mystery that stirred something deep in his memory, yet remained just beyond his understanding.

Lukas rose to his feet. As he began to make his way toward the park's edge, he turned to look back at the bench where his friend lay. Through the upward-drifting snow, now settling as a gentle shroud over Tonto's still form, he glimpsed something that made him pause.

A figure emerged through the mist—tall and ethereal, mounted on a white horse that moved with unearthly silence. The rider appeared to shimmer, as though clothed in armour that caught light from another realm entirely, though the details wavered reminiscent of a heat mirage. It was as though time itself had slowed, the rider advancing in almost slow-motion, each movement flowing into the next with such grace and an almost instilling beauty that deepened the already profound silence of the park. The rider's presence commanded a reverence that hushed even the deathly quiet a million times over, creating a pocket of stillness within stillness.

The horse's hooves made no sound against the snow-covered ground, its passage as quiet as falling snow itself. The deathly silence that surrounded them felt sacred, venerable, as though this moment existed outside the ordinary flow of time.

As the figure neared the bench, a singular star began to glow in the skies above Kennington Park. Its twinkle, though weighted with solemnity, brought at least some form of comfort that would persist and be there for his journey back home.

Lukas smiled and nodded at the star, a knowing salute to the celestial witness of this moment. With a final glance at the shimmering rider and his fallen friend, he turned from the scene, the mark on his palm pulsing gently as he made his way toward the edge of the park.

As he walked, winding through Arcanum's shifting landscape, the realisation of what he must do crystallised in his mind. Peter would be waiting—had always been waiting—for this final confrontation. The mathematician who had created this mirror version of London from his desperate need to escape reality's cruelties. Lukas understood now that defeating Peter wasn't about battle or magic; it was about helping him see what Tonto had shown Lukas: that running from reality only created beautiful prisons.

The streets began to change around him, sometimes familiar, sometimes bewildering, leading him inevitably toward the place where it had all begun. Not a bridge between worlds, but a moment of choice between two ways of seeing the same world.

Dawn painted the sky in desperate shades of crimson as Lukas reached the point where Arcanum's illusions were strongest. Here, reality wavered reminiscent of heatwaves, the buildings twisting in ways defying comprehension, the very air shimmering with mathematical equations made manifest. The Thames flowed in confounding arrangements nearby, sections moving upstream while others rushed

THE SUN RISES

toward the sea, creating whirlpools that shouldn't exist.

His heart still ached from Tonto's transformation, the weight of the tortoise's final moments pressing against his chest comparable to a stone. The white cascade continued its upward dance around him, each particle catching the blood-red light of sunrise.

"Such a transformation need not be permanent," came a voice that appeared to emanate from the very equations that held Arcanum together. "Stay, and what you've lost can become something new again."

Peter materialised before him, his form shifting between states—one moment a being of shadow and fractured light with obsidian wings that stretched across the width of the street, the next a gaunt man with hollow eyes and ink-stained fingers. This was the first time Lukas had seen Peter's true human form—the lonely mathematician who had discovered Arcanum's equations and lost himself within them.

"I know what it's like," Peter said, his voice suddenly stripped of its supernatural resonance, becoming the weary tones of a man who had calculated himself into isolation. "To feel connected to something, then watch it slip away."

His human eyes—grey as November rain—held a desperate loneliness that made Lukas's heart constrict with unexpected compassion.

"Stay here, where nothing need ever truly end."

For a moment, Lukas could see the human Peter had once been—a brilliant mind who had glimpsed configurations others couldn't see, who had retreated into his equations when human connections proved too painful or complex to navigate. In that haunted gaze, Lukas recognised something of himself—the same retreat into music when reality had become too harsh, the same desire to create perfect motifs to compensate for life's messiness.

"I can give you wonders beyond imagining," Peter continued, his form expanding once more into something terrible and beautiful, wings of obsidian light casting shadows that moved against the direction of the

185

sunrise. "A world where death is merely a transition, where loss can always be reversed."

The ascending snow danced between them, each particle a tiny mirror reflecting what could be. Peter's offer was almost overwhelming, a siren's call to his deepest desires. In the swirling white, Lukas could almost see Tonto alive again, could almost feel the warmth of his presence.

"You never understood, did you?" His voice was quiet but steady, surprisingly resolute in the face of such immense power. "Tonto's sacrifice wasn't about escaping reality through magic. It was about truly seeing reality—all of it. About being fully present in every moment, whether wonderful or terrible."

Peter's form flickered, the human mathematician momentarily visible again, his face contorted with pain and longing.

"Reality is cruel," he said, his voice breaking. "I calculated the precise mathematics of suffering. I quantified the exact equations of loss. Reality is merely the cruellest of all possible dimensions."

"No," Lukas said gently, seeing Peter—truly seeing him—perhaps for the first time. "Reality is where love matters precisely because it doesn't last forever. Where connections mean something because they can be broken."

Peter's beautiful, terrible form resumed, wings beating against the dawn, but now Lukas could see the frightened mathematician hiding within the majestic illusion.

"You would choose to see London only through mundane eyes again? Exist without magic?" Peter's voice shifted between supernatural resonance and human desperation.

Lukas smiled through his tears, a genuine, heartfelt smile that reached his eyes. "There's magic in London—there always has been. Arcanum isn't somewhere else; it's here, woven into every brick and cobblestone. Tonto showed me how to see both at once. His love wasn't about lasting

THE SUN RISES

forever—it was about showing me the truth."

As he spoke, the mark on his palm—Tonto's final gift—warmed slightly, pulsing with quiet assurance. It wasn't flashy magic, just the subtle comfort of connection that transcended worlds and even death itself. This was what Peter could never understand—that true magic wasn't found in spectacle but in genuine bonds freely given.

"I spent 40 years," Peter said, his human form briefly emerging again, "calculating the perfect equation—a mathematics of reality that could undo suffering." His voice cracked. "No one should have to endure what ordinary reality demands of us."

In that moment, Lukas saw Peter not as an enemy but as a brilliant mind broken by the very problem Lukas himself had faced—how to reconcile the wonder and cruelty of existence, how to find meaning in a world where everything precious eventually ends.

"The perfection you're searching for," Lukas said gently, "it doesn't exist. Not even here." He gestured to Arcanum's unnatural architecture. "You've created a beautiful illusion, but it's still just running away."

Peter lunged forward, his form spreading akin to spilled ink across the street, his power threatening to engulf Lukas. The obsidian wings beat the air, creating a chilling soft breeze that smelled of sulphur and regret.

"Then stay here in pain! Stay where every moment reminds you of what you've lost!"

But Lukas stood his ground, feeling Tonto's final peaceful moment in his arms, understanding at last the profound lesson the ancient tortoise had imparted. This wasn't about escaping grief; it was about understanding its place in the tapestry of life.

"Love doesn't need to cross between worlds when there's only one world to begin with—seen through different eyes," Lukas said, his voice echoing across the street that existed in both London and Arcanum simultaneously.

Peter's scream shattered windows along the street, a sonic wave of frustration and defeat. But its power washed over Lukas without effect, bouncing harmlessly off the shield of his newfound understanding.

In that moment, he saw clearly—the being before him was nothing but fear given form, the terror of accepting life's imperfections, the desperate clinging to a world where loss could be undone, where reality could be bent to avoid pain.

"You have no power over me," Lukas said softly, his voice filled with compassion rather than defiance. "You never did. The real magic was always in here." He pressed his hand to his heart, feeling the echo of Tonto's love resonate within him. "In accepting both the joy and the pain. In loving despite knowing we'll lose. In seeing wonder in the ordinary."

He thought of the marketing campaigns he'd created that had felt most meaningful—never the technically perfect ones, but those born from real emotion: the narrative he'd crafted during the painful months of his sister's illness. The works where imperfection and humanity had been allowed to show through had always felt most authentic to him.

Peter's magnificent form began to dissolve, wings turning to mist in the morning light. For a brief moment, only the man remained—thin, pale, with ink-stained fingers and haunted eyes.

"They called me mad," he whispered. "Said my equations were unfathomable. But I solved them. I found the place where reality bends."

"And lost yourself in it," Lukas said gently. "Found a perfect world but couldn't bring your humanity with you."

"It will be lonely without you," Peter admitted, his form growing translucent. "So few understand the designs."

For the first time, his smile was genuine, human, touched with sadness rather than malice. "Perhaps there is a theorem I missed. An equation of imperfection I failed to calculate."

THE SUN RISES

"Maybe there's no equation for that," Lukas replied. "Maybe that's the whole point."

As the sun broke fully over the horizon, bathing the street in golden light, Peter's form appeared to come to a decision. His eyes fixed on Lukas with a new clarity, the desperation slowly giving way to understanding.

He reached into the pocket of his weathered jacket—now fully human, the obsidian wings and supernatural darkness having receded completely. From it, he withdrew a small nub of chalk, worn down by years of use. Lukas could see faint mathematical notations embedded in its texture, complex equations and formulas that had once mapped the pathways between worlds.

"This," Peter said, his voice now entirely human, carrying the weight of decades of isolation, "is the last thing I brought with me from the other side. The chalk I used to first calculate the equations that opened the door to Arcanum." He turned it over in his fingers, revealing an almost invisible series of numbers and symbols etched into its side.

"All this time, I've kept it. When everything else from my human life faded—memories of family, of friends, of who I was before—this remained. My link to what I once was." His voice cracked slightly. "My final tether to the mathematician who thought he could solve the universe's cruelty through pure logic."

He extended one hand—human now, with age spots and paper cuts from years of mathematical work—and pressed the small nub into Lukas's palm.

"For the configurations you might still wish to understand," he said, his voice fading as his form began to disperse comparable to morning fog. "Some questions are worth pursuing, even without perfect answers."

As the chalk touched Lukas's skin, he felt the fundamental shift occur. The air around them shimmered and twisted as Arcanum's unnatural geometries began to unravel. Peter's final act of selflessness—giving up the one thing that had anchored him to his mathematical paradise—had broken the equations that held this mirror world together.

"Thank you," Lukas said softly, understanding the enormous sacrifice this simple gesture represented.

Peter's form was barely visible now, just a human outline in the morning mist. "Perhaps," he whispered, his voice already distant, "you were right. Perhaps the perfection I sought was never in the equations at all."

With those words, he dissolved completely into the golden light of dawn, not vanquished but transformed, finally releasing his desperate grip on both his illusion and reality.

The world around Lukas shuddered, not so much changing as revealing its true nature. The twisted architecture of Arcanum didn't disappear—it settled, revealing itself to have always been London, just seen through the lens of mathematical impossibility. Fish that had been swimming through air merged seamlessly with the Thames below, their scales still occasionally flashing with light when viewed from certain angles.

Buildings that had writhed with Peter's influence now stood as familiar London structures, though Lukas could still perceive subtle movements when he looked with his newfound vision. A gust of soft breeze whipped across the street, carrying the scent of diesel and coffee, yet within that ordinary breeze, Lukas could now detect configurations and whispers of what he had known as Arcanum—not gone, just integrated into his perception of London as it had always been.

Lukas noticed that where Arcanum had been most powerfully manifested, ordinary London now showed subtle differences—not magical distortions, but whispers of what he now understood lay beneath all reality. A lamp post leaned at a slightly more graceful angle, a section of pavement formed a more perfect curve, a wrought-iron gate displayed slightly more organic motifs in its design. Not Arcanum imposing itself on London, but Lukas's perception revealing the hidden elegance that had always been there.

The ascending snow ceased, leaving only ordinary snowflakes drifting downward through ordinary air, a gentle reminder of the extraordinary events that had just transpired.

Lukas stood on the familiar London street as normality returned, feeling both heavier and lighter. Heavier with the weight of his grief, but lighter with the understanding he had gained, the lessons he had learned, and the love he would carry with him forever. From the shell in his shirt pocket, he could still feel a phantom warmth where Tonto had pressed against him in those final moments. Not magic, but memory. Not power, but love.

The mark on his palm—the configuration from Tonto's shell—had faded to become barely visible, The morning crowds began to pass by, commuters hurrying without noticing anything unusual, their faces etched with the mundane concerns of daily life. But Lukas saw differently now. He saw the way sunlight created halos around hurrying figures, the way the river's surface reflected the sky in a constantly shifting mosaic, the magic hiding in plain sight in every ordinary moment. He saw the potential for kindness in every face, the hidden beauty in every corner of the city.

He turned toward home, ready at last to live in a world where real magic didn't need cards or spells or alternate dimensions. It just needed open eyes and an open heart.

As he walked down the street, a bell tolled, its sound crisp and clear, belonging wholly to London. The air shimmered around him. The last of the morning mist curled around his ankles—ordinary fog with no trace of Arcanum's shimmer. He could have sworn he felt a familiar presence beside him, not the weight of Tonto's physical form but the warmth of his lasting influence, guiding him still.

He looked back one last time at the spot where Peter had stood, now just empty pavement in an ordinary London street. In his pocket, the small nub of chalk remained—a reminder that some questions were worth asking even without those perfect answers.

London had never looked more extraordinary— The warmth of a beautiful morning radiated through his body as he noticed how the early sunlight caught the ripples of the river in geometric designs whilst Pigeons traced perfect arcs through the air that reminded him of the unnatural angles he'd witnessed in what felt akin to another world, countless times before.

The morning continued to unfold around him— traders setting up their stalls, early church bells calling to service, excited voices from the morning's school run carrying on the soft breeze. Each moment was touched with its own kind of magic, and now Lukas could see both aspects simultaneously: the London that everyone saw and the Arcanum that had always existed alongside it. The bells rang with overtones only he could hear, and the light falling across the stalls revealed geometries that most would never notice.

Lukas walked on through his city changed not by magic but by love. He understood that London and Arcanum weren't separate realms but different facets of the same reality, and the greatest magic was the courage to see this truth and to love deeply, even knowing that all things, eventually, come to an end.

14

Fortunes Told

The morning light felt different. Lukas stood on the corner of Kennington Park Road, where the Victorian terraces cast their familiar shadows across the pavement. Everything was exactly as it should be – the newsagent's metal shutters rattling upward, the sound of the 133 bus wheezing to a stop, the smell of coffee drifting from the café on the corner. And yet. His writer's eye caught the subtle stories of ordinary existence – the shutters rising akin to the opening line of a tale, the bus's air brakes releasing in a sigh that punctuated the sentence, the conversations creating configurations that would have once appeared random but now revealed perfect structure. He realised with startling clarity that Arcanum hadn't been a separate world at all, but rather this same world viewed through a different lens—comparable to seeing ultraviolet or infrared spectrums suddenly revealed. The magic hadn't been there; it had been here all along, hidden in plain sight, woven into the very fabric of ordinary reality.

He pressed his palm against the rough brick of the building beside him, needing to feel something solid and real. The texture was correct, properly rough and cool against his skin, but he couldn't shake the sensation that if he pressed too hard, his hand might sink straight through. This wasn't a magical effect but a psychological aftershock – his brain still adjusting to the certainty of physical laws after experiencing their suspension.

A woman hurried past, her heels clicking a precise rhythm on the pavement. In the old world – the normal world – he would have barely noticed her. Now, he couldn't help but see how the morning light caught in her hair, creating a momentary halo that reminded him of The Star's celestial glow. He blinked hard, forcing himself to see only what was actually there: a tired commuter clutching a paper coffee cup.

"Right then," he muttered to himself, pushing away from the wall. "Get on with it."

But every step felt wrong without the gentle scratch of claws beside him. No Tonto. The thought struck him akin to a physical blow, making him stumble slightly. A passing teenager grabbed his elbow.

"You alright, mate?"

"Yes, thanks. Just... lost my balance."

The teenager nodded and moved on, but Lukas noticed how his shoelaces glowed slightly in the morning light, one orange, one blue. He squeezed his eyes shut. When he opened them, they were just ordinary white laces.

Absently, his fingers found the mark on his palm—the design from Tonto's shell that had transferred to him during those final moments in Kennington Park. It had faded to a faint outline, evocative of an old scar or birthmark, but it still carried a subtle warmth when he focused on it. Not magic, exactly, but a tangible reminder that his extraordinary journey had been real. Occasionally, he would find himself subconsciously tracing the design with his thumb and find clarity amongst his thoughts arising not from supernatural guidance, but from a deeper connection to his own intuition—as if Tonto had awakened something that had always been within him, a wisdom that needed no magical realm to exist.

He made himself walk forward, past the local shops he'd known for years. The greengrocer was arranging apples in neat, orderly rows. The bakery's steam rose in shapes that almost formed letters before dissipating. Or did it? Everything familiar had taken on a dream-like quality, as if reality itself had become gossamer-thin.

A black cat sat on a garden wall, regarding him with venerable eyes. For a moment, Lukas's heart leapt – but no, this was just an ordinary cat. Not a guide. Not a friend. Just a cat enjoying the morning sun.

"I suppose I should be grateful," he said aloud, earning a strange look from a passing dog-walker. "At least the pavement stays where it should be now." But part of him missed the unconventional angles of Arcanum's streets, the way buildings would lean in to whisper secrets, the stones that would shift under his feet reminiscent of living things.

As a bus passed by, its windows created a warping effect of light and shadows across the café front. Lukas caught a fleeting glimpse of what looked akin to a man with a mathematics journal. Something in the distorted reflection—a posture too still, too composed—made his heart skip a beat. For a moment, he thought he looked up, and eyes that conveyed too much knowledge, too much age for an ordinary face met, looking directly at him through countless layers of glass. Then the bus was gone, and with it the unsettling image. Lukas blinked, uncertain if his mind had conjured Peter's visage from lingering anxieties or if some echo of the man truly lingered between worlds. Not a threat, not any more, but a reminder that some doors, once opened, never fully close again.

His fingers brushed against the small nub of chalk in his pocket—Peter's last connection to his human life, freely given in that final moment on the bridge. The chalk felt ordinary to the touch, yet somehow weighty with significance. Lukas decided he'd always carry it with him, a tangible reminder that even the most lost souls could find moments of redemption, that the most complex equations sometimes resolved in the simplest acts of selflessness.

Inside his house, everything was exactly as he'd left it, whenever that had been. Time felt slippery in his mind. How long had he been gone? The calendar on his kitchen wall still showed April, but appeared oddly out of place, as if from another time. Had the seasons changed without him noticing, or had time itself become distorted in his mind?

His mobile phone lay on the kitchen counter, its screen dark. He pressed the power button, half expecting it to display mysterious symbols or start speaking in riddles. Instead, it simply showed the date and time: 7:42 AM, 2nd May. Ten missed calls from James.

James. The memory of him as The Magician flashed through Lukas's mind – brilliant, dangerous, beautiful in his power. But that wasn't real. The real James was probably worried sick, wondering where his boyfriend had disappeared to over the bank holiday weekend. The James who had stayed up all night to help Lukas work through those band promotions, bringing fresh tea every hour on the hour. The James whose methodical precision balanced Lukas's creative chaos so perfectly, creating a harmony between them that no magical realm could replicate.

Lukas's hand hovered over the phone, but he couldn't bring himself to pick it up yet. How could he explain? "Sorry I missed the weekend – I was in an alternate dimension where all our friends were Tarot cards come to life, and my tortoise guide died saving me from the Devil"? Yet even as doubts crowded his mind, he picked up the phone. Whatever happened in Arcanum had taught him one thing clearly – real connection, with all its imperfections and complications, was infinitely more valuable than magical illusion. James deserved the truth, or at least as much of it as Lukas could express. Perhaps not everything needed explanation – perhaps it was enough to say that he had been lost but now was found, that he had finally understood what James had been telling him all along about the beauty in imperfection, about the music they created together simply by existing in the same space.

His fingers moved decisively across the screen: "I'm home. I've seen something extraordinary. Can you come home? There's a story I need to start writing, and I want you to hear it first."

Lukas's phone rang almost immediately after he sent the text, James's voice tight with concern and relief.

"Thank God, I've been worried sick. Where the hell have you been... I've been out of my mind!"

"It's... complicated," Lukas replied, smiling despite himself at the inadequacy of the word.

"I'm coming home. Now. Don't you dare disappear again".

An hour later, James stood in his doorway, hair dishevelled, eyes bloodshot from lack of sleep. He studied Lukas's face with the careful attention he usually reserved for architectural blueprints, noting every subtle change.

"You look... different," he said finally. "As if you've aged years in days."

Lukas took a deep breath. "I experienced something beyond comprehension. Something I can't fully explain without sounding completely insane." He led James to the living room, sat him down. "But I'm going to try, because what happened has changed everything about how I see the world. How I write. How I understand us."

James, ever the rationalist, looked sceptical but nodded. "Start at the beginning."

Lukas made himself a cup of coffee, the mundane routine of measuring beans and heating water helping to ground him in reality. The morning light streamed through his kitchen window, casting ordinary shadows that stayed exactly where they should. A sudden movement caught his eye – just a paper napkin shifting in the breeze from the heating vent. But for a second, he'd seen it as one of The

Fool's dancing scarves, twirling with gravity-defying grace through the air.

The coffee maker beeped, startlingly loud in the quiet kitchen. Lukas poured himself a cup, watching the steam rise in its familiar, ordinary arrangements. He took a sip – Did it taste of starlight and midnight storms, of unfathomable journeys and venerable magic? No. It was just coffee. Good coffee nevertheless, but just coffee.

He walked to the front steps, needing to see the morning crowd, to remind himself of normal life. The usual parade of commuters streamed past – suits and trainers, headphones and newspapers, all the familiar sights of a London morning. But now he saw more.

He saw how the businessman's tie rippled reminiscent of a banner in a wind no one else could feel. He noticed the way the school children's laughter hung in the air akin to visible notes of music. He watched the sunlight catch on windows across the street, turning ordinary glass into portals of possibility.

"Stop it," he told himself firmly. "That's not real any more."

But wasn't it? Hadn't Arcanum simply shown him what was there all along, hidden beneath the surface of things? The magic hadn't gone away – he was just seeing it differently now.

A pigeon landed nearby, pecking at nothing on the clean pavement. Lukas watched it, remembering how Tonto would eye the birds with timeless wisdom in his gaze. The grief hit him fresh and raw – not just for Tonto, but for everything he'd lost. The wonder of Arcanum, the perfect understanding of his transformed friends, the pure magic that had flowed through every moment there.

But he hadn't really lost it, had he? The magic was still here, in the way morning light painted the walls golden, in the perfect spiral of steam rising from his coffee, in the synchronised dance of commuters weaving past each other without collision.

Weeks later, Lukas sat at his writing desk, fingers moving rapidly across his keyboard. His first novel – a magical realism piece inspired by his journey – was taking shape with surprising speed. His marketing career transforming into a writing one, using his industry contacts to arrange meetings with literary agents who'd shown interest in his sample chapters.

A small gem-like piece of Tonto's shell, extracted from where he'd carefully wrapped it in silk and placed it in a drawer, now sat mounted in a simple frame above his workspace - the one physical memento he had of his extraordinary journey. Rather than a painful reminder, it served as a touchstone, a connection to the wisdom Tonto had shared and the perspective Lukas had gained.

Beside it, placed carefully on a small stand, sat the worn nub of chalk that Peter had pressed into his hand that final morning. Its surface still bore faint traces of complex equations—the mathematics of crossing worlds—now faded comparable to distant memories.

Mike and Sarah sat on the sofa behind him, listening as he read his latest chapter aloud. They remembered nothing of their time as Arcana, but something in his writing appeared to resonate with some deeper part of them. Sarah occasionally touched the silver bracelet on her wrist she'd found in a local antique stall. It reminded her of something but she wasn't sure what—though she'd developed an uncanny intuition about people's emotions since that weekend, sensing their hidden truths as if moonlight revealed what daylight concealed. Mike would tilt his head in the exact manner of The Fool when certain passages were read, and had lately embraced a spontaneity that surprised even himself, finding wisdom in impulses he once would have dismissed. Sometimes they would exchange glances during Lukas's reading, as if sharing a private joke they couldn't quite remember but felt on the tip of their tongues. These unconscious gestures and unspoken exchanges confirmed what Lukas had come to understand—that while Arcanum itself might be gone, its essence remained, integrated into the fabric of ordinary reality for those with eyes to see.

"It's as if you're translating a different language," Mike said when Lukas finished reading. "But somehow I understand it perfectly, even though I couldn't explain why." He started to say something else, then stopped, as if grasping at a thought just beyond reach. "It's odd— sometimes I dream I'm falling, but I'm never afraid. I just feel... this incredible freedom."

Sarah nodded in agreement. "It feels akin to remembering something I never actually knew." She touched her bracelet absently. "Last week, I found myself standing by the river at night, just watching the reflection of the moon on the water. It felt as if I stayed for hours, as if waiting for it to speak to me." She smiled uncertainly. "That sounds mad, doesn't it?" She leaned forward. "Will you submit it to be published? People need to read this."

"James is helping me revise it," Lukas confirmed. "Though he says I need to prepare for both acclaim and confusion. Not everyone will hear what you're hearing."

"Their loss," Mike said with a shrug. "It's bloody brilliant. Unlike anything I've ever read, but somehow exactly what stories should be."

The late afternoon sun cast long shadows down Portobello Road as Lukas approached number 291b for what he somehow knew would be the last time. The shop's façade had returned to its familiar dilapidated state – peeling paint, clouded windows, and that perpetual air of abandonment that had first drawn his curiosity. Yet something was different.

Through the grimy glass, warm lamplight spilled out, catching dust motes that danced reminiscent of fallen stars. Inside, Cassandra moved with deliberate grace, her silver hair catching the light as she methodically cleared shelves and packed away curiosities into boxes that appeared to absorb far more than their dimensions should allow.

Lukas pressed his palm against the cool glass, remembering Tonto's weight in his arms during those final moments in Arcanum. The venerable tortoise's sacrifice had taught him more about love and magic than all the unfathomable wonders of that other world.

The bell above the door remained silent as he pushed it open. The shop's interior felt smaller now, more confined by the laws of ordinary space, yet somehow more magical for its limitations. Every object held stories – real ones, human ones – that needed no supernatural enhancement to be extraordinary.

"I wondered when you'd return," Cassandra said without turning. She was wrapping what appeared to be a Victorian music box in brown paper. "Though I suppose 'return' isn't quite the right word. You never really left, did you?"

Lukas smiled, running his fingers along a shelf edge. "No, I suppose I didn't. Not in the ways that matter." He picked up a small mirror, studying his reflection. The face looking back was his own, yet transformed by understanding rather than magic. His eyes had the same depth and wisdom he'd seen in Tonto's gaze – not supernatural but the natural result of profound experience.

"You knew, didn't you? About Tonto, about everything?"

Cassandra finally turned, her eyes holding the same ageless wisdom they'd shown on that first day. Her movements followed the same deliberate rhythm they always had – efficiency refined to its purest form, creating the appearance of preternatural grace through simple economy of motion. "I knew what needed to happen. Just as I know what needs to happen now." She gestured to the boxes and half-empty shelves. "All doors must close eventually, so new ones can open."

"What about Peter?" he asked quietly, the name feeling strange on his tongue—giving the entity that human name still felt akin to a concession, an acknowledgment of the complexity behind the role of adversary.

Cassandra's hands paused momentarily over her wrapping. "He

was human once, you know. Brilliant, sensitive, too perceptive for his own time." Her eyes held something resembling compassion. "Some souls find themselves caught between worlds—too aware of the arrangements behind reality to be content with ordinary existence, yet too attached to humanity to fully transcend it."

Lukas reached into his pocket, fingers brushing against the small piece of chalk—a mathematician's tool, Peter's final connection to his humanity. "He gave me this. His chalk." He held it up to the fading light filtering through the dusty windows. "Said it was the last thing he had from his human life."

Cassandra's eyes softened as she looked at the worn nub. "That was the key, you know. In the end, it wasn't your triumph over him that restored balance—it was his choice to surrender the one thing that still connected him to his former self. That small act of selflessness, giving up the tool he used to first calculate the equations that opened the door between worlds..." She smiled gently. "Sometimes the greatest magic comes from letting go."

"Will he find peace?" Lukas wasn't sure why he cared, after everything Peter had done, yet he did.

"Perhaps. Your encounter changed him too, you know." She smiled enigmatically. "Not all who wander between worlds are lost forever."

"What happens to Arcanum now?" Lukas asked, realising he needed to know that the realm hadn't simply disappeared. "Is it destroyed forever?"

Cassandra's smile held layers of meaning. "Arcanum was never a place, Lukas. It was a perspective—a way of seeing reality's hidden dimensions. Those who need it will always find their way there, just as you did." She placed a gentle hand on his arm. "But it changes form, adapts to what each seeker needs most to learn."

"And the others—Mr. Richards? Katie? all those who became Arcana?"

"They've returned to their lives with perhaps a slightly enhanced awareness, small echoes of who they became there. You might notice Mr. Richards' advice becoming more eerily prescient, or Katie developing an uncanny intuition. Small gifts from their time as something more than themselves." She looked around the shop. "Transitions are never clean, Lukas. Boundaries blur, energies exchange. That's where the real magic happens."

Lukas reached into his jacket pocket, fingers brushing against the familiar edges of the tarot deck. He pulled them out, spreading a few across his palm. Though they appeared ordinary enough—ink and card stock, nothing more—something about them had subtly shifted. The Magician's face now carried a hint of James's determined expression. Justice reflected in Sarah's gentle eyes. The Fool danced with Mike's particular energy and grace. Not obvious enough that anyone else would notice, but unmistakable to him. The cards remained still in his hands, no hint of the power they once channelled, yet they appeared to have absorbed impressions of those who had embodied their archetypes.

"The cards," Lukas said, looking up from his examination. "I should return them."

Cassandra shook her head. "Keep them. Though I suspect you'll find you don't need them any more. The best fortunes are the ones we create ourselves, moment by moment, choice by choice."

"Will I see you again?" Lukas asked, though he already knew the answer.

"You'll see magic everywhere now," she replied, her gentle smile confirming his intuition. "In the way sunlight catches on windows, in the kindness of strangers, in the quiet moments between heartbeats. That's better than seeing me, don't you think?"

Outside, the street lamps were beginning to flicker to life, their warm glow mixing with the dying sunlight to create extraordinary colours that reminded Lukas of Arcanum's ever-changing sky. A young couple walked past the shop window, laughing at some private joke, their shadows stretching and merging in ways that appeared to defy the laws of physics.

She moved to the door, picking up an old brass key from the counter. Its metal caught the light, momentarily flashing with the same otherworldly gleam that had once filled Tonto's knowing eyes.

"It's time," she said softly, moving to lock up for the final time.

Lukas stepped outside, turning to look through the dusty window one last time. Cassandra stood framed in the fading light, her figure somehow both solid and ethereal. Their eyes met in perfect understanding – both knowing that the real magic had never been in the cards or even in Arcanum's unnatural geometries, but in the way they had changed his vision of the ordinary world.

The shop's windows darkened for the last time, but Lukas smiled, knowing that every street in London now held wonders for those who knew how to look for them.

Later that evening, Lukas leant against the kitchen door frame, watching as James carefully prepared dinner. Since his return from Arcanum, they had finally made this house their home. James chopped vegetables with the same precise, measured movements he'd once used to conjure doorways between worlds – though he had no memory of that time. Still, traces remained: the way his fingers would sometimes trace unfamiliar designs in the air when he was thinking deeply, the occasional flicker in his eyes when the light caught them just so.

"What are you staring at?" James asked without looking up, somehow sensing Lukas's gaze.

"Just admiring the view," Lukas replied with a smile.

James glanced up, his expression softening. "How's the novel coming along? Hit any walls today?"

"Actually, I finished the first draft." Lukas moved into the kitchen, placing his arms around James's waist. "It's rough, but it's there."

"That's brilliant!" James turned, pride evident in his eyes. "We should celebrate. I've been saving that bottle of Malbec."

As they moved around the kitchen together, Lukas marvelled at the comfortable rhythm they'd established. What they had wasn't the dramatic, world-altering connection he'd experienced with The Magician in Arcanum. Instead, it was something more precious – a deep, steady love built on genuine understanding, on accepting each other's flaws and gifts equally.

"I saw Sarah today," James mentioned as he stirred the sauce. "She's wearing a silver bracelet that looks exactly as you described in your book – the one The Moon wears. Odd coincidence."

"Is it?" Lukas asked, smiling to himself.

James gave him that look – part exasperation, part affection. "You and your magical thinking." His hands moved with precise, measured movements as he prepared dinner, unconsciously tracing geometric designs in the air as he reached for herbs and spices. "Though I will admit," he added after a moment, "sometimes when I'm designing, I see connections in structures that I can't entirely explain. Solutions that feel akin to... remembering rather than creating." He shrugged it off. "Professional intuition, I suppose." He placed a hand on Lukas's shoulder, squeezing briefly. When he withdrew his touch, a slight smudged handprint in chalk remained, though neither of them noticed.

"I love it," Lukas countered.

"I love you," James corrected, then paused. "Even when you talk about tortoise spirits and living Tarot cards."

They ate dinner by candlelight, sharing stories of their day. The mundane details – a difficult client, a frustrating commute – appeared just as magical to Lukas as any of Arcanum's wonders. The imperfections, the small irritations, the undramatic reality of loving someone day after day – these were the true magic he'd been searching for all along.

After dinner, Lukas sat at his desk, adding final notes to his manuscript. His fingers moved across the keyboard with confidence, shaping words that might help others see what he now saw – the extraordinary nature of ordinary existence. The story wouldn't capture everything – some experiences transcended artistic expression – but it would be honest in a way his previous work never had been.

As night fell completely outside his window, Lukas continued to write, the words flowing with newfound freedom. The narrative grew and evolved, incorporating elements that would have appeared unfathomable before his journey—temporal shifts, voices that shouldn't work but somehow did, silences that spoke as eloquently as words.

It wasn't perfect. Nothing truly valuable ever was. But in its flawed, human beauty, it captured something essential about both worlds he had inhabited—and the understanding that they had, in fact, always been one and the same.

About the Author

David James is a storyteller who brings the same sense of wonder to his fiction that drives his creative studio, Adventures of the Persistently Impaired (...and Other Tales). Before diving into the world of writing, David spent nearly two decades in the music industry, working with major labels like Universal Music and EMI Records-an experience that infuses his stories with authentic cultural references and a pulse on what resonates with young readers.

His journey as an author began unexpectedly through a *different* Fortunes Told project, where he created unique Tarot-inspired designs for fashion that evolved into a narrative universe that young adults and adults alike could explore through both physical items and digital experiences. This blend of traditional storytelling and interactive elements reflects David's belief that the best stories exist both on and off the page.

With characters who navigate life with neurodivergent perspectives, David draws subtle inspiration from his own experiences with ADHD. His writing features protagonists who turn their perceived differences into unexpected strengths, often discovering magical or technological solutions to everyday challenges.

When not writing, David can be found experimenting with new technologies, developing creative tools to help other storytellers, and adding to his collection of vinyl records.

For more, visit http://www.othertales.co

www.ingramcontent.com/pod-product-compliance
Lightning Source LLC
LaVergne TN
LVHW090056080526
838200LV00098B/393/J